3 1116 00647 7084

D0108724

LOOP
HOLE

ROBERT POLLOCK

A NOVEL

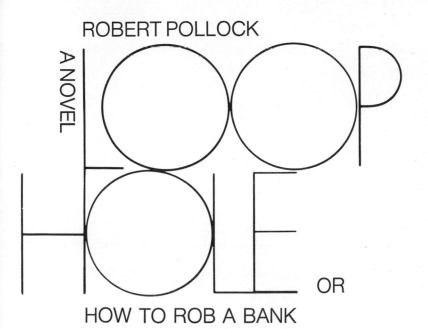

LOOP
HOLE

OR

HOW TO ROB A BANK

E. P. DUTTON & CO., INC. | NEW YORK | 1973

Published simultaneously in Canada by Clarke, Irwin & Company Lim-
ited, Toronto and Vancouver

SBN: 0-525-14865-5

Library of Congress Catalog Card Number: 72-94699

To my mother

Most authors would agree that there are times when without the support of some very special people they would have floundered and perhaps sunk. This author wants to express his gratitude to those who gave him more than the practical help he asked for: Eve and Leslie Kark, London, England.

There is nothing so degrading as the constant anxiety about one's means of livelihood. . . .
Money is like a sixth sense without which you cannot make complete use of the other five.

Somerset Maugham
Of Human Bondage

Mike Daniels crouched over the safe. A thin, concentrated beam of light cut through the blackness and lit the keyhole of an old one-ton Chubb safe.

The tall, thin man was holding the flashlight, and a third man, whose job was to tack up the black felt curtains that kept the light and sound in, stood by the window.

In the warm, still night you could hear the distant rumblings of overnight trucks speeding on the now clear, fast lanes of the North Circular. In the warehouse a black cat tensed. Her belly brushed the rough wooden floor and her tail lashed with soft fury. She could hear the scratchings the mice made as they played between the freshly boxed eating apples.

She had watched the three men when they had walked into the warehouse and had even rubbed herself against the leg of one of them. But they were too intent and had no time to waste flattering her.

Mike worked with the calm, unhurried precision of a professional. His hands were strong and the fingers that pushed the plugs of gelignite into the keyhole were long and wasted at the knuckles. They held a knitting needle that gently prodded the explosive into the hole, like a surgeon's scalpel.

"Always do like watching him work, don't you?" the thin man said. He was careful to keep the light steady. Mike enjoyed the compliment. He looked up at the long, dark figure. "Nothing to it, really." He smiled. "Not much anyway." His hand went to the jacket pocket of his suit and pulled out a small detonator that he carefully pressed into the gelignite in the keyhole. He taped it over and secured it to the safe door. Then he wrapped the wires from the detonator around the handle of the safe and let them uncoil onto the floor. He stood up and studied the results of his work.

"Right then, that should do it. You can cover up now."

The thin man gave him the flashlight and started to cover over the detonator and keyhole with handfuls of putty he took from a black plastic bag.

"Funny stuff," said Mike. "You got to watch it. It's like fat old men, sweats with age. Only the sweat from gelignite is pure nitro; very unstable."

The other man was finished and he too stood away from the safe.

"Got the sacks?"

The short one came away from the windows and started to drape the safe with the sacks they had soaked in the office girls' washroom. Mike trailed the detonator wires across the floor of the office to the back of a large desk on the far side. When the safe was covered, the two men went over and lay with him behind the desk.

There was a muffled roar and the room vibrated. A

metal filing cabinet drawer opened as if an invisible hand had pulled at it. In the depths of the warehouse the cat leaped onto a string-bag mountain of Brussels sprouts and crouched there in fear.

"It hasn't gone," said Mike.

"How the hell can you tell that?"

"You get to know the sound."

They came up from behind the desk and Harry, the third man, went through the settling dust to the safe. He tried the handle. It did not move.

"Fuck it."

Mike looked up and grinned. "Why not?" he said.

The thin man grinned back at him and reached into the inside jacket pocket of his suit. He brought out a packet of Durex prophylactics.

The men went back to the safe and Mike inspected the keyhole that was now an open, jagged orifice.

"Better file the rough edges, Harry," he said. "Don't want to rupture anything."

When the hole had been filed wide and smooth, Mike took one of the Durex and opened it out. Then he fed it gently into the gaping keyhole. He held the ring end and started to drop the small plugs of gelignite into it. He waited after each piece to check that it had slipped down into the contraceptive. By the time he had used what he knew would be the exact amount of explosive, the Durex was hanging down on the inside of the safe door like a soft drooping penis.

He took another detonator from his pocket and

placed it in the ring end of the Durex. He taped it to the safe door and stood away again from the other two who puttied it over.

"I think we'd better have something a bit more substantial than wet sacks this time."

"What about having the full ones?" said Harry.

They filed out into the warehouse and together dragged sacks of potatoes back into the office. They stacked them around the safe until it looked like a mound growing out of the floor. When they were satisfied that the insulation was sufficient, they went back behind the desk again and waited for Mike to detonate the explosive.

"Here we go," he said.

This time the noise was much louder, and as the safe door crashed open the sacks of potatoes split and spewed out over the office floor.

"Jesus," said Harry. "Instant mashed."

"Get the bags," Mike said.

They moved quickly and together like a team. The safe door hung limply on its hinges and inside they could see the neatly stacked bundles of notes. Mike reached into the safe and emptied the money onto the floor. The other two waited and packed it into the tough plastic bags.

Their mood was light and they swapped banter as they worked. They had the confidence of men who had worked together before, who knew one another's capabilities and felt secure about them. They had opened a safe and were getting what they had come for.

"How much did he say there was in here?" Mike asked them.

They kept working. "Fifteen to twenty grand."

"I told you he exaggerated."

"They're all the same. They get carried away."

"There's got to be ten," said Harry.

"Feels more like seven."

The safe was empty. Mike pushed the door back but it would not close anymore.

"They'll be needing a new one I fancy."

"Wonder how much they'll say we nicked?" said Harry.

"At least three or four grand more than what's here. Make a nice little profit on the insurance I shouldn't wonder."

They were careful not to tread on the scattered potatoes as they crossed the office to the door that led into the open warehouse. They walked to the main door down the narrow, dark corridors made by the stacked boxes of fruit.

"Got the key, Harry?"

He took a bunch from his pocket and unlocked the door. The unloading yard was clear.

As they passed through the door the tall man, Gardner, glanced back. "They'll be belling the place after this I would reckon."

Mike checked his watch. "Yeah, well those nice security men should be along in about three minutes. So don't let's hang about."

Harry was at the high mesh gate. He opened it, using

a key from the bunch, and edged onto the street. It was still and quiet. He beckoned the other two and waited until they were out and then he relocked the gate.

They walked in single file, each carrying two bags of money, along the line of parked cars until they reached a gray 3.8 Jaguar. Harry opened the driving door and climbed in. Gardner went to the front passenger seat.

Mike passed his two bags through the open window so that all of the money was now in the front where they could grab it in case they had to abandon the car.

"My place in about an hour," he said. "An' don't get done for speeding, old Bill's very severe on bad drivers in this manor."

The Jaguar pulled slowly and smoothly away from the curb. At the end of the road it made a right turn across the North Circular and headed toward Hanger Lane.

Mike buttoned the jacket of the dark suit that had been tailored for him in Soho and walked casually after the Jag. He crossed the main road and walked on into the maze of suburban side streets with their neat rows of uniform houses.

In the warehouse the black cat pounced. There was a quick flurry and then she lay with her front paws stretched out holding down her prey.

Mike's flat was on the fourth floor of a development in South London that had won its architects an award—not that any of the architects actually lived there.

In one of the two bedrooms his children—Darrin, a boy of five, and his three-year-old sister, Kate—were asleep. Life in the flat revolved around the living room with its huge color television set and the kitchen where, when they were not watching the box, the family ate. It was a very well-equipped kitchen with a washing machine, a dishwasher, a refrigerator and food mixers. The modern, expensive labor-saving devices were really too much for its size, and Doreen, Mike's wife, had to squeeze herself to make and serve the tea for the three men who sat at the yellow formica-topped kitchen table. It reminded her that she had not kept to her diet.

As she waited for the electric kettle to boil, she looked first at the pile of money on the table, then at the men. She always felt a great relief when Mike came back after a night's work. He was brown from lying in the sun during the day and she thought he looked very handsome and strong. Gardner never looked fit: he was too long and thin with long hollows in his cheeks. Harry, she thought, was very comical. Probably because he was the short, fat one of the three and was very sensitive about going so bald at his age. He was twenty-nine.

Mike looked over at her and smiled.

"It won't be long," she said. "Nearly boiling."

"No sugar for me, love," Harry told her.

She said she remembered and they both laughed.

"Well, that seemed all right," Mike said. "How much you reckon for the other fella?"

Gardner thought about it. "Not as much as he figured. He didn't get it quite right, did he?"

Mike weighed a packet of notes in his hand. "This okay with you two?" They looked at the packet, then at each other, and mumbled an agreement.

He went to a drawer in the kitchen cabinet, took out an envelope, put the money in it and sealed it over. He put the envelope on a shelf between a box of detergent and some rolls of toilet paper.

"I'll see he gets it," he said.

"Not much room here, is there?" Doreen giggled. They pushed the notes away and she was able to put the cups of tea on the table in front of them.

"I bet you're well pleased, aren't you?" Harry said.

She laughed again. "You don't have to ask."

Mike sat stirring his tea. "Why don't you pack off to bed now, love."

"What and leave you with all that loot?"

Mike looked up from his tea. She had learned the signs. He wanted to talk business. "All right then," she said. "I'll be off."

"Don't let the kids wake me. I want a nice long kip."

Harry got up from his chair, put his arm around her shoulders and gave her a theatrical kiss on the cheek. "Very nice cuppa tea, darlin'."

"Good night, Harry." She laughed. "An' you Gardner."

When she had gone from the room Harry turned to Mike. "You're bloody lucky you are."

"Yeah, I know," he said. "Anyone for more tea?"

"I'll have some." Gardner passed his cup across the table. "You got anything else in mind?"

Mike didn't want to answer him right away so he pretended not to hear and went on making fresh cups of tea. He had a sense of the dramatic and he wanted the scene set to his own advantage. In his mind he had been over the conversation, inventing the questions he guessed the others would raise and developing his answers. He wanted to excite them, to persuade them to agree, but at the same time he didn't want to tell them too much—not yet—not until he was certain.

He poured the boiling water over the tea bags, added the milk and then carried the cups to the table. When he was seated and comfortable and ready he looked over and, as if answering the question, said, "I've been thinking."

Harry stopped his continual stirring. "You always was a great thinker."

"Ever heard of the City Savings Deposit Bank?"

"Jesus! You got to be kidding." He knew as he said it that Mike wasn't the kind of man to joke. Not about business anyway.

"It can't be done," Gardner told him. "A lot of firms have thought about it. You just couldn't pull it off. Even if you got in you couldn't get out."

"No?" Mike let the question out slowly and deliberately.

Harry nervously took a packet of cigarettes from his pocket and offered them round.

"No thanks," Mike said. "They're bad for the chest." Then he continued. "I can get you in and I can get you out."

Gardner drew on the cigarette. "Speak for yourself, mate. That place is so tight you'd have the law round your neck before you could move."

"He's right, Mike." Harry was excited now. "They've got vaults even you couldn't blow and what about the security? The blokes what do them don't clock in on the hour."

"I know what they got. I know every foot of that place. I'm telling you I can get in and out and I won't be caught."

"What you mean, you won't be caught? You're talking like you're all set to do it."

He leaned back in the chair. "I'll tell you, mate. I am."

Harry stood up. "I gotta have a pee."

When he had gone Gardner leaned across the table of money, shortening the distance between them.

"You really serious?"

"I just need the right people."

"How much is in there?"

"Between one and three million."

Gardner let the breath come through his puckered mouth in a silent whistle. They heard the water flush in the bathroom and they waited.

Harry closed the door behind him and looked from one to the other.

"Now what's he said?"

"That there's upward of a million in them vaults."

"Christ! I mean think of what they'd say in the papers."

Mike waited for the tea to settle. "Well, what do you think?"

"I still don't believe it."

Mike got a bottle of scotch and poured three glasses. "I got two kids and a woman sleeping in there. Liberty is a great institution an' I don't reckon to perpetrate a job that's going to end up with me seeing 'em once a bleedin' month across a visiting table."

He passed the glasses and they drank without calling a toast.

"There's months of planning gone into this. You wouldn't even need to do another job. You wouldn't have to. It's what everybody dreams about, only they never get to doing it."

"How many would we need?"

He knew he had them; now it was "we."

"Us and another three. Plus the straight guy I've been working on."

"What straight guy?" Gardner said. "I don't like having anyone on a job who's straight."

"He's technical and necessary. Everybody was straight once, even you."

The first part of it was over now. They were into the planning without realizing it.

"I want a nice, quiet firm," said Mike. "No temperament. You talk to Taylor. Make a meet with him. He's got two mates who're supposed to be good."

"They'll want to know more." The long face was sullen again.

"You just tell him who it is, Gardner."

Mike poured three more drinks and this time they raised their glasses. "Here's to it, then," said Harry.

None of them seemed to consider the neat piles of money on the table. They might have been slabs of cheese they had brought home instead of the cash equivalent of an M.P.'s yearly salary.

"I figure we'll need four grand to finance it," Mike said, looking down at the table.

"That still leaves some for spending." Harry was smiling.

They cleared the table of the cups and the glasses. As if to make a final confirmation Mike said, "Shall we count it out then?"

Gardner picked up the first bundle and started to count the notes, one by one. "It's all right by me," he said.

Stephen Booker was made redundant three weeks before Christmas.

The season, naturally, carried emotional overtones, but as he felt strongly about the total commercialism of Christmas it did not hurt over much: it was not being at the office party that was the major disappointment. He had had plans for that. Now there would be no lunch that stretched into late afternoon before the evening festivities got under way. The party was for employees only; it did not include wives, husbands or boy friends. So, he spent the time at home with his wife, wrapping presents.

They had given him what he had called "a tin handshake." Six months' money and a reference that in spite of its euphoric recommendations damned him. If he were that good, why spring him onto a market that was already full of unemployed geniuses?

As it turned out, his job—that stablemate of middle-class respectability—was only worth six months' capital.

He could not understand why they had let him go. He was a good architect; he knew that. It seemed that somehow it had always been his assignments that hit snags with clients who pushed for more than they deserved. But when he really thought about it, he knew that was not true. Everybody had problems—how a man deals with them is what is important.

Most of all, was the rejection. The excuses they gave you didn't count. You are finished and one day after lunch you have to clean out your desk and collect your instruments in the open-plan drawing office while the other men, the friends you worked with, try not to look.

Then you all put on a façade and play out the embarrassment of hearty good-bys and bad jokes.

At four thirty in the afternoon you are standing on the pavement in the cold and it is easy to drive home because the rush of people with jobs has not yet started.

He was spending a fortune on stamps, mailing endless applications to companies that advertised in the professional columns of *The Daily Telegraph, The Sunday Times* and his own trade paper, the *Architect's Journal.* He went to see the professional headhunters, who called themselves placement consultants, and filled in their pages of questions and talked to their psychologists. He found that being forty-five and without a degree were two handicaps that no amount of form filling and ego spilling could compensate.

He discovered that the urgency of his position was something the firms he wrote to failed to understand. Most of them didn't even bother to acknowledge his application. Of those that did, more than half sent a printed postcard telling him he was being considered, invariably followed by duplicated notices of rejection, weeks or even months later. The others, the minority and usually the small businesses, invited him for an interview.

At first the interviews were enjoyable. He had the confidence of enough money in the bank to carry him. He was easy with the man on the other side of the desk, chatting with him, swapping stories. He would pick and choose the firm to work for, the model of car supplied, the expenses. But either he did not get the jobs or they were not good enough for him. It was still early enough to be selective.

"Give it three months," his friends had said. "Plenty of time to look around before deciding." It was easy to say when expense accounts were paying for the midday beer.

As the weeks and then the months drifted away, his pace slowed. The New Year's promise and then its anticlimax depleted his energy. His weekly schedule became geared to the days when the best advertisements in the newspapers were published. Time seemed to jump. Suddenly another week had vanished.

He became involved in housework and in taking and collecting his two daughters from their small, private school. Because there was no monthly infusion of new money, the thought of their tuition became a nightmare. You didn't have to be an accountant to see that what was left of his savings and handshake money would be devoured when the summer term became due.

By the fourth month he was becoming conscious of

his wife's silent observation of how he filled his time. If he took too long reading the morning papers, while she busied herself in the house, he would feel her resentment. She wanted action. The guarded, helpful suggestions she made at the beginning about the situations vacant she read in the papers gave way to cryptic jabs. "Nothing good enough for his lordship today I suppose?"

He was a neat and orderly man and did not, until the pressures began to affect his health, look forty-five. His face became thin and haunted and his suit began to sag on the body that, at one time, he had been proud of. It even seemed that his thick, dark hair was becoming lifeless and flecked with gray. "You're losing your looks," Jennifer told him, which was very reassuring.

Jennifer Booker tried to understand. She was perceptive and sensitive enough to know instinctively that his pride was being attacked. That it was necessary for him to keep his confidence and self-respect. But in spite of this she found herself doubting him. Why had he been fired? Why hadn't he been taken up by another firm of architects? Was he perhaps not as good as she had once believed?

It began to affect her physically and she made excuses in bed. In the early months they still allowed themselves a drink and a bottle of wine on weekends. He would buy half or even quarter bottles and pour them into whole ones that they kept, in case anyone came round for a drink. She would start off wanting him, because of the drink, but even his touch seemed to lack confidence. He needed to be held and caressed. It took him longer to become excited and this created a lack of response in her. His body on hers was heavy because his muscles no longer tensed and flexed with the lightness and power of lust.

He accepted her excuses too easily. He agreed and turned over in their bed and with the crutch of a sleeping tablet sank into a sleep he knew would not be interrupted by the ringing of an alarm clock. There was no need for him to get up early anymore.

The bank manager studied Stephen Booker's statement. "I do understand your problem, Mr. Booker," he said.

He turned a page. "Ah, yes. We have a second charge on the house."

"It's increased tremendously in value," Stephen said. "Wimbledon's a very good area. I've been offered nearly double what we paid."

"Ah," said the bank manager. He put the papers into the buff folder. "Don't suppose you've thought of selling and taking the profit?" The lean, thin face smiled at Stephen across the desk.

Booker felt a surge of ease. "Well, of course it would give me tax-free about seven thousand pounds."

"Yes, but I don't think we've quite reached that stage yet. When can we anticipate seeing further funds?"

"Well"—this was the tricky part—"I'm short-listed for three senior positions and . . ."

"Nothing definite then?"

"Well, no. Not quite."

The bank manager pursed his lips and leaned back in his chair. "I'm afraid the bank can only support you for another month Mr. Booker. You're overdrawn this morning to the extent of, let's see." He consulted the buff folder again. "Two hundred and forty-eight pounds."

"I'm sure the position will regularize itself," he said.

"Good," said the bank manager.

They both stood up. The inquisition was over. They didn't use thumbscrews anymore, not ones that you could see.

"I'd hide that checkbook if I were you." The mouth and its smile were practiced and oily.

"Yes," Booker joined in the joke. He knew the form.

Jennifer and the girls had gone to see his mother-in-law and he sat alone in the chic comfort of the sitting room, which he had spent so many do-it-yourself hours perfecting, and decided it was all over. He studied the French hand-block wallpaper and admired the way the red- and yellow-flowered pattern on the brown background matched so symmetrically, roll to roll. As good as any professional could have done it.

He had used his architect's taste and knowledge to shape their house until he hoped it reflected something of their family personality. But his personality had been sapped by his failure. He had not fulfilled the promise of his youth when he was brash enough to boast about the startling career he would carve from the mediocrity of the world of architecture.

Somehow it had always been someone else who was lauded as the new talent. He was always just a few steps behind, but it was those few steps that made the difference. As a creative business talent, as a husband and even as a father he had not delivered. Provided, but not delivered. There was no fur coat hanging in the closet or Aston Martin in the garage. There were substitutes that were almost acceptable—almost.

Their house, in Wimbledon, had a mortgage that was just a little too high to be comfortable. The building society had been delighted to give him the loan. Four months of payment arrears had changed that attitude. Even the patience of Harrods had finally and very justifiably run out.

Stephen was an optimist and somewhat of a fatalist. Something always turned up at the eleventh hour. But the old reliable pattern had let him down and while his income diminished the creditors accumulated. It became a pathetic equation.

It seemed to him that the bank manager, credit associations, private schools, medical care funds and his wife and home had become monsters who were bleeding him.

His wife couldn't accept the situation and when he actually got down to it, neither could he. They were part of a system in which failure was the end of everything; the front was the only meaning. When the summer came, Jennifer started the familiar feminine campaign of wanting things. She had nothing to wear. The campaign began slowly and gathered and gained in frequency and momentum until it seemed to him that her whole mentality was taken up by the way she looked.

He forgot that it was the way she was that had attracted him. She was a woman whose looks improved with age, her olive skin and fair hair gave her an outdoor aura of freedom and appeal. The lines looked good on her face. Her body was slim and her legs were long and moved beautifully.

"You want me to look attractive don't you? Then provide. That's what husbands are supposed to do, remember?"

He hated her. She had no logic. She never listened.

"You'll have to wait. Why can't you learn to wait?"

"I've waited long enough and for what? For you to sell the house? Well, it's not good enough. Do something. Get out and earn for a change. I'm telling you, Stephen, sell this house and you're on your own."

"It would be a new start," he told her. "With the profit there'd be no more debts and money in the bank."

"Oh, fine," she said. "And where would we be stuck? Out in the back of beyond vegetating with no friends. I'm not starting all over again. Find another way. Get some money for Christ's sake. Other men do."

Finally everything she said, however ordinary, carried a cutting edge. "The girls need new shoes." "I have to pay the milk bill." "We're out of tea bags." His mind ached with the demands. They drained him and nobody would believe or understand that in spite of the fine car, which he fed in half-gallons, or the house with its long overdue mortgage repayments, there was no more money. That he couldn't go to the bank anymore; that there was nothing left for him to sell or even pawn.

She didn't know. In his panic he couldn't see that her mind was taken up with the falling apart of everything that represented her security. They were in a blind, vicious circle, gnawing at each other.

He began to understand why some men committed murder.

The green and black Librium capsules that his doctor prescribed calmed him from the brink of paranoia, but they could not remove the demands or rekindle the creative urge.

So he sat and decided that he would kill himself. He had always joked that he was worth more dead than alive. It was the epitome of modern social advancement. He had his first really good laugh for months. That would fix his bloody bank manager.

There was pleasure in the self-pity the thought gave him. Jennifer would feel the full force of the guilt—he liked that idea. Then he thought of his children. He could accept the final failure of suicide but what about them? What would they be told? What picture of him would they grow up with?

37

Depression and drink combined and he wept. He sat with his head in his hands and let the warm tears run down his face and into his mouth so that he could taste the salt. He began to wonder how to do it. Gas, he thought. No pain—just off into a quiet sleep forever. He stood up; there were preparations to be made.

Halfway to the door he stopped. "Shit." It came out as a loud cry. "Shit. It's North Sea gas, not lethal. You can't do it that way anymore."

Standing in two neat rows on the formica-topped kitchen unit were a line of capsules and behind them a line of white tablets that he knew contained barbiturates. The bottle of whiskey still had a couple of good slugs left. If the newspaper reports were right, the combination would be fatal.

The wall telephone rang as he sucked back the second capsule. It was probably Jennifer. He let it ring but then the incessant tone got through to his neat, logically trained mind and he picked up the receiver.

"Hello."

"Hello, Stephen. Tony."

"Ah, Tony."

"How goes it? Still one of Britain's vast army of unemployed?"

"Yes, but not for long. And you?"

"No, back in the land of the living. I got a part at last. A play, start rehearsals next week."

"That's great Tony," he said and he meant it. The poor sod had been resting for months.

There was a pause and Stephen cradled the telephone receiver under his chin and stretched out to take another capsule.

"Stephen, you still got that four-door car?"

"Yes," he said. "Jennifer's taken the train to her mother's this time."

"Good. I've got a great idea. I'm coming off the circuit. You take my place. I haven't told 'em yet so the job's yours for the taking."

Stephen surprised himself by laughing. "What you mean, become a mini-cab driver?"

"Why not, for Christ's sake? I did. God, at least it'd keep you going. I was picking up forty quid a week, cash."

He held the third capsule in the palm of his hand.

"As much as that?"

"Yes. If you do nights, at least you can have the afternoons free for interviews."

"It's something to think about," he said.

"Don't be so bloody soft, Stephen. There isn't time to bugger about. I'll fix it. You still got a decent driving license?"

"Yes, I think so."

"Great. That's it then, I'll give the office a ring. Now how's everything else?"

"Oh, not bad," he said.

"Fastline, one-nine. Where are you, one-nine?"

"Kensington High Street—over."

"Customer in office. Make base—over."

"Roger, roge. Out."

It was nearly midnight and the traffic was thinning away. The office of Fastline was down a side street off Holland Road. It was in a shop that had once been a workmen's café. The front was painted a bright yellow and over the glass doorway was a neon sign that said "Fastline Cars. 24-hour Service."

The linoleum on the floor was pitted with cigarette burns and in the corners were empty tins of engine oil, Coke bottles and old car batteries. Against the two facing walls were the wooden chairs the drivers used when there were no passengers waiting. By three in the morning the drivers would be lolling in them, some trying to sleep, others gathering for a poker game, the room thick with cigarette smoke.

The third wall was a pine partition with a counter; behind it sat the controller. He took the telephone calls and gave out the jobs, either over the radio or to the waiting drivers. There was a strict rotation. Behind the door in the partition was another door which led to a smaller room with a gas stove, a bathroom, a basin and in a corner an old sofa the night staff used in the dead hours of the morning. It was only big enough for one and the unlucky had to catch their sleep on the chairs in the outer office.

The place was used and dirty in spite of the efforts of the owner to smarten it up with large wall maps of

London with the best routes marked out on them in red ball-point ink, but even so, there was a good feeling when you returned to base. There was always a slight excitement about the next job; the camaraderie with the other drivers; stories to swap about passengers too drunk to find their money, or women who wanted their luggage carried beyond the door of their flat, quite willing to pay waiting time.

Nobody asked him for a reference or reason or his car insurance. He could drive, his car had four doors and it ran. They sold him a heavily thumbed copy of the *Geographier's Guide to London* and taught him how to use the two-way radio they fitted to his car. He was a mini-cab driver.

Without realizing it, he was becoming part of a community again and he told himself that since all of them needed money to survive, Fastline was more real and true than the office he had once shared with his educated, status-conscious contemporaries.

"How are you, man?"

"Billy," Stephen said. "Your wife came round looking for you."

The face grinned. "I just been home an' given it her."

The controller looked over at the big, lumbering man.

"Billy, you're a black bastard you are."

"If I be a white man I be a white bastard too." He laughed.

"One-nine," the controller said. "Twenty-five Passington Court. Going to Waterloo and you're five minutes late already so get a bleedin' shift on."

"Twenty-five Passington Court," Stephen yelled back through the glass entrance door. "Any bell?"

"No, she'll be waiting outside."

He cut off Kensington Road and took the one-way system behind Olympia. The woman was standing on the pavement looking very agitated so he gunned the car and screeched to a stop.

"Mini-cab, ma'am?" he said.

"Oh, my God. Yes. Where have you been?"

He jumped out, took her suitcase and opened the passenger door in one practiced action. He didn't answer her until he was back in the driver's seat moving away from the curb.

"Had an urgent call for some blood." He lied. "Very busy tonight." In the rearview mirror he watched her adjust her skirt and get comfortable.

"Blood? What do you mean blood?"

They were easing through High Street and the road looked clear. If he could beat the lights at Church Street it would be an easy run.

"Well," he said, "we carry blood samples for the hospital group. Always very urgent. What time's your train?"

"What train?"

"I thought you wanted Waterloo."

"Oh, no. Plane. West London Air Terminal."

"Ah," he said, and downshifted before he made the right turn into Gloucester Road.

"One-nine, are you P.O.B.?"

The woman jumped. Stephen reached for his hand mike.

"Only our radio," he told her.

"Roger. Passenger on board, Fastline. Fastline, this passenger for West London not Waterloo."

"Roger, roge, one-nine, better try a convert then, hadn't you?"

He put the mike back into the glove compartment.

"Going to Heathrow, are you?" he said to the woman.

"Yes." She was being very cool with him, to show her annoyance.

"I could drive you straight out. Only cost another pound over what you'd have to pay on the coach."

She thought about it. "All right then, why not."

He reached for the hand mike again.

"Fastline, one-nine."

"Come in, one-nine."

"Convert London Airport."

"Well done, one-nine."

Twenty-five minutes later he was climbing the curved concrete ramp that lead up to terminal one.

"Here we are then, safe, sound and on time."

He came out of the car very smartly and opened the door for her. Then he brought out her suitcase.

"Two-fifty all together," he suggested.

She handed him three one-pound notes and he made the slow effort of hunting for her change.

"No," she said. "That's all right."

"Oh, thank you very much," he said, trying to sound surprised. "Have a safe trip."

"I hope so," she said.

He hung by the car for a minute hoping to pirate a straggling arrival or even an air hostess, but a taxi came up the slope and he decided not to take the risk. They could be very nasty at the airport about mini-cabs.

The weeks of driving for a living had given him a professional smoothness. He could always tell when passengers were impressed and it pleased him. At the end of his twelve-hour shift he emptied out the ashtrays and wiped down the black, leather-finished upholstery. He carried a perfumed aerosol can so that his other passengers would not flinch at the stale smell of cigarettes or drink.

Jennifer had invented a story for the girls so that they thought the reason for their father being out all night and having a two-way radio in the car was just slightly dangerous and romantic.

Because he slept for most of the daylight hours and left the house immediately after their early dinner in the evening, the relationship between them improved. It was, he thought, because they saw less of each other. There wasn't the time to generate a row.

Part of her, the woman, admired him again for doing

something, but the wife was embarrassed. She worried constantly that he would pick up someone they knew as a passenger.

"How long do you think it will go on?" she asked him.

"I don't know. It's better than sitting around all day."

"I think you're getting to like it."

"Not really. At least it's bringing in some cash. What with that and the dole it's almost possible."

"Until the car breaks down. All those miles, it can't be any good for the car."

"I don't flog it," he said.

She was right though, he was doing over two hundred miles a week and it was their own car he was driving, not a company car that didn't matter.

He bought some pieces of fried chicken from the all-night take-away shop in Shepherd's Bush Green and then cruised slowly back to the base. The office windows were steamed up and as he pushed through the door he could see they were playing poker.

"Eating again, one-nine?"

"I bought some extra," he said.

"He's lovely he is." The man was sitting on the controller's side of the counter, holding his cards close to his chest.

"I suppose you all want some tea?"

"One-nine, you're telepathic."

45

He counted them. Six including Polish the controller. They handed him their tea-stained mugs. The water was cold and the drying-up cloth was wet but then hygiene was hardly a major factor at Fastline.

"Who's got the sugar?"

"Why don't you bastards buy some for a change?" Polish reached down to his private cupboard and unlocked it.

"It's the day drivers. A load of bloody thieves."

The light on the telephone box started to flash.

"Hold it down," said Polish.

He picked up a receiver and flipped the switch on the box. "Hello, car service."

Some of the men were still laughing and Polish put his hand over the mouthpiece. "For Christ's sake, belt up."

"Sorry, sir. Where are you?"

He wrote the address on a small pad.

"Going to?"

"Oh, yes, I know. Be there in five minutes."

Polish put the phone down and then tore the slip of paper from the pad and folded it once across the middle.

"Who's next?"

The men look at each other and one with very long, dark hair, who never seemed to bother about wearing socks, said, "I am, but let one-nine have it or we'll break up the game."

They all nodded.

"Right then, here you are, one-nine." Polish handed

the slip of paper to Stephen who opened it out and read the scrawled instructions.

"The pubs are closed," he said.

"That Daniels?" said the man who did not wear socks.

"Yeah," said Polish. "Just ring the bell at the side door and he'll come out."

"He tip me a fiver once," said Billy.

"Well, it looks like he's not doing any trips tonight," said Polish. "Straight home to Battersea."

"What's he do?" Stephen asked him.

"Christ knows, but it must pay him well."

"Get a move on, one-nine."

The pub was on Goldhawk Road on the corner of one of the succession of small, dark side streets that ran off it. Booker hated going into the pubs along that road. In fact he hated the whole district. It always seemed full of drunken Irishmen.

He wondered what sort of man was still in a pub at three in the morning. He backed into the side street, left the engine running, got out of the car and rang the bell. In his nervousness he smiled to himself and thought it was like a getaway car. A dog barked in the pub. It was loud and deep throated and sounded like a German shepherd.

The door opened and a man stood in the light from the hallway. Stephen could not see into the hallway from his angle, but he could sense the dog.

"Mini-cab, sir," he called.

"Be right with you," the man said.

He slid behind the safety of the steering wheel and waited. The man came round behind the car and Stephen leant over the seat to open the passenger door for him but the man ignored it. "I'll sit in the front," he said.

The car moved into Goldhawk Road and headed toward the green.

"You're new aren't you?" the man said.

"Relatively," said Stephen. "Been on for about six weeks now."

The man watched him drive and studied him. The creased but good-looking sports jacket, the turtle neck sweater and his hands. The nails were short, clean and well cared for.

"What were you doing before?"

Stephen changed gear as he approached Hammersmith Broadway.

"I was an architect."

He changed up and passed an overnight truck.

"Now I'm an unemployed one."

"Bit tough in that game is it?"

The lights at Cadby Hall changed to red and Stephen eased the car to a stop. He turned and for the first time got a decent look at his passenger. He was somewhere in his late twenties, healthy and good-looking with tight, thick, curly hair that grew over his shirt collar. The suit looked well cut and expensive. The lights changed and they moved away.

"It's the economic climate, a reduction in spending capital for new buildings."

"Oh, yeah. What sort of buildings were you doing?"

"Office blocks mainly," said Stephen. "A lot of work in the City at one time."

They were coming up to the junction of North End Road and West Cromwell Road and the lights changed against them again.

"Some nights you can't go wrong," said Stephen.

"Don't worry son, I'm in no hurry. Know the City well, do you?"

"Yes, pretty well."

"Must be interesting. Ever find anything, you know, old ruins like that?"

"No," Stephen told him and the lights changed. They didn't speak again until they were in the Wandsworth Bridge Road.

"How much you reckon to do driving the cars?"

"Well," said Stephen, "not enough, that's for sure."

"Gets a bit tight does it?"

"More than a bit."

"Yeah. Take the next left, then over the road an' we're there."

The car slowed down as it reached the skyscraper blocks of Council Flats.

"Anywhere here'll do," the man said.

He reached into his hip pocket and took two pound notes from his wallet.

"Here, keep it."

"Oh, thanks very much."

"My name's Daniels. I move around a lot. Don't like using my own motor much, so I'm quite a customer of

49

your people. What's your name? We could have another little chat sometime."

"Booker, but if you ever want me just ask for one-nine." He smiled. "We all have code numbers."

"Yeah," said Daniels. "Come in very useful they can."

He gave Stephen a half wave and then walked away across the open car park.

Over the next three weeks it seemed that Daniels called for Stephen every time he moved around London at night. The drivers even started making jokes about it.

Stephen liked him. He was what his own friends would call, in their acquired patronizing way, a rough diamond.

Their conversations tended to be staccato one-way affairs with Daniels putting most of the questions, like a gentle, sympathetic inquisitor who just wanted to know.

It suited Stephen, who by nature was a listener. At last he had found someone in whom he could confide; someone he could unburden himself to who did not criticize all the time. He found that although he told Daniels almost everything about himself during their journeys together, there was very little he had learned about his passenger. His name was Mike, he had a wife and two children and he never seemed to be without a lot of money. But how he got it still remained unanswered. Not for any particular reason but because Stephen had never actually come right out and asked.

The evenings were warm and it was light until quite late. Daniels rang for him around nine, as the darkness was beginning to come. Stephen made the familiar journey to Battersea in good time and waited by the open-air car park that had been laid out by the planners of the estate.

Mike Daniels came walking out into the open space and Stephen realized that he didn't know just exactly which block he lived in or the number of his flat.

"Hello, Stephen," he said, climbing into the passenger seat. "How are you?"

"All right. The girls went back to school today. Makes the place nice and peaceful for a change."

"What about those fees you have to pay?"

"Well," he said, "I was wondering about them myself."

He took a breath and let the air out in a sigh. "Where to?"

"Just let's have a little drive. Something I want to ask you. Go along the South Bank through to Blackfriars, then over the bridge an' down into the City." Mike looked out at the deepening sky. "Should be a nice drive this time of night."

Stephen slipped the car into gear and moved out into the main stream of light traffic that was moving east.

"Ever thought what it is I do?" asked Mike, sitting with his shoulder braced against the door.

Stephen looked straight into his young, tough face. "Yes. I was going to ask you actually."

"I'm a thief."

He couldn't help laughing. "You're a what?"

"That's right, a thief."

"Oh, I see."

"Yeah, I bet you do."

"Give me a minute or two. I mean it's not every day one meets a self-confessed criminal."

"Watch the road. You nearly shot a red light just then."

They reached Vauxhall Bridge before either of them spoke again.

"What exactly is it you thieve?"

"Money mostly and the odd piece of tom—jewelry."

"From old ladies' bed-sitters?"

Mike smiled at him, holding back the offense he felt. "Now that wasn't very nice, was it?"

The gears seemed rough and they grated as he changed down at the Parliament Square roundabout.

"What did you expect?"

"I said I was a thief, not a bleeding thug."

"What, until somebody gets in your way?"

"The way I work people don't get the chance. I'm a peterman." He spoke the words with pride. "An expert with safes."

Stephen took his eyes off the road.

"Have a good look," said Daniels. "You won't find no mark of Cain."

"Why do you do it?"

He laughed. "Because I like the money, that's why."

"Well, there are other ways."

"What, like driving mini-cabs? You don't pull a grand a week that way, mate."

Stephen's foot came down heavily on the brake pedal and the car almost skidded to a stop at the Blackfriars Bridge lights.

"How much?"

"You heard. And I'm not putting it on either."

"Why are you telling me? It's not exactly wise going around boasting like that, is it?"

Mike settled back in his seat. "I don't have to boast," he said. "You never had the feeling you'd like to relieve a bank of some of its liquid assets?"

"Sure and spend the next few years in jail. No thanks."

"That only happens if you're foolish enough to get captured. Head for Cannon Street."

There was very little traffic on the City roads and they drove in silence. Stephen was trying to handle and analyze the shock Daniels' revelation had given him. He adjusted quite quickly to the sudden knowledge that the man was a thief, and it didn't somehow seem terribly important. It was the suggestion that in himself he too might consider the idea, that his reaction had been a qualification and not an outright denial. He wouldn't rob a bank because he might get caught, but did that mean that if the risk was negligible he would?

"Take the next left."

There was a feeling of tension in the car.

"Now the second on the right. Pull up about here."

The road was wide and almost empty. Stephen could make out lines of office blocks with shops at ground level. The area had not been totally redeveloped and there were old buildings standing next to new, white slabs of glass and concrete.

"Don't kill the engine."

Stephen felt the tightening of the nerves in his stomach. He turned to Daniels. "You're not going to . . ."

"Don't be bloody silly," he said. "Just having a look around."

He sat and waited, a taut, strung-out, upright body at the wheel.

"See that building over there?"

Stephen looked across the road. "The old one with the dark brown brickwork?"

"That's the one."

"Yes."

"It's a bank, right?"

"Yes."

"Called a carrier. Heard that before?"

"No, I haven't."

Mike Daniels was smiling and relaxed. He wondered what was going through the architect's mind. One more step forward would be enough for now, he thought. Give him time, time to think about it, about what it could do for him. Sow the seed and let it germinate on its own.

"Well, I'll tell you," he said. "They have about one to four million in their vaults."

"Good Lord," said Stephen.

"Let's hope so," said Daniels. "Naturally the vault is down in the basement. Under the ground, as it were."

Stephen turned. "Impregnable I would have thought."

Mike laughed. "Yeah," he said. "That's right. Only I'm going to have some of that loot. You can drive me back home now."

"I'm just going over to the common for a walk."

Jennifer Booker looked at her husband over the flat top of the kitchen unit. "You're up early."

"I've got someone to see," he said.

"What, on the common?"

"No, in the pub."

"That sounds more like it," she said. "Little social visit?"

He stood by the open front door frowning. "It's about a job, believe it or not."

"Oh, dear me. Don't say we're going to get a job."

He slammed the door without bothering to reply.

She nearly threw the plate after him. "I'm going mad," she cried. "Bloody, bloody mad."

He skirted the pond where some children were fishing for tadpoles and headed for the windmill. This was it, the day he finally had to make up his mind. In or out—

there was no in-between, no compromise. He had suggested to Daniels that maybe he could act as a sort of backroom adviser, but the man said that wouldn't do. He would have to be there: it was that critical.

He tried to add it up in his mind. Supposing he was offered a job, what then? It would be too late. But it was almost too late anyway. The writs had started to arrive.

His whole edifice, everything that had been achieved over the years, was going to fall about his head.

The high, white windmill was just ahead, and on the road leading to it Stephen saw a navy blue Rover 2000 slowly moving toward the car park. He recognized the driver.

The arrangement was that Daniels would catch up to him; it would look like two men out for a walk on a sunny afternoon.

The paths were worn smooth and because of the good weather they were hard, almost slippery. He used to bring the girls here with him when they were younger and would explain about the trees and insects and the frogs and tadpoles in the pond. It was the nearest he would ever get to living in the country. If Daniels' plan worked, perhaps everything would change and life would become easy again and there would be time for enjoyment instead of the constant nagging, worry and fear that ate into his stomach.

He heard footsteps coming up behind him but he didn't turn. There were other people on the common.

"Very nice up here."

He felt a sense of relief at the sound of the familiar voice.

"Yes, it is. You're prompt."

"Well," Mike said, "it's only polite."

"Do you want to sit by the pond or walk?"

"Oh, let's have a sit down," Mike said.

"I wasn't sure how you did this sort of thing."

Mike laughed at him. "Bit like James Bond, is it?"

Stephen managed to smile back at him. "Well, not really," he said.

They sat on the carved wooden bench and looked at the water in the pond.

"How's everything at home?"

"It hasn't changed," said Stephen and then he was off, letting it all come out again because there had been no one else to tell.

Mike Daniels listened. Occasionally he would look up from the water and into Stephen's face to see the lines of worry that had become etched into it. He wanted Stephen to talk to him like a father confessor so that the bond between them would become deeper.

"If I just had a couple of thousand. It's capital I need; not a lot, but all at once, a lump sum."

"That's what we all want," Mike said.

"I might be forced to sell the house at last. What happens when they make you sell your home?"

"You sell it and buy another one."

"I couldn't. She'd leave me."

He had come to the end now and they both sat in

silence. When he was ready, Mike turned to him and said, "Have you thought about it?"

"I don't know," said Stephen.

"You're still worried about being nicked, aren't you?"

"Of course I am."

Two elderly ladies, out for their afternoon stroll, came toward them.

Mike looked up at them as they passed and smiled. They smiled back at him.

"I keep telling you we won't get caught," he said to Stephen.

"How many times has that been said?"

"This is different, really different. You know enough to see that for yourself."

Stephen stood up and went to the edge of the pond and sat down on his haunches. "How long did you say it would take?"

Mike smiled. "Twelve hours, maybe."

"That's a long time."

"It's a lot of bleeding money."

As if to make a final effort to convince himself that this was the only acceptable solution, the only way out left to him, he asked the one question that he had repeated at almost every meeting. "No violence?"

Mike tried to hold back his impatience. "Who are we going to get violent with? We're not rushing in and blowing a load of rice at the ceiling for Christ's sake."

Stephen came back to the bench and sat down. Then he made his decision which, like most decisions of any importance, had been made a long time ago. The questioning and the justifications were not really part of making up his mind: he needed them so that he could tell himself how difficult it had been and that circumstances had forced the action upon him.

"All right."

"You're in then," said Mike.

Stephen looked away. "Yes," he said. "Yes, I'm in."

"No change of mind or anything silly like that?"

"I said yes."

"That's all right then," Mike said.

He reached into the pocket of his sports jacket and brought out an envelope. "Here. Put this away."

Stephen took it from him and felt its texture in his hand. "What's in it?"

"To help you relax. Always think better when you're relaxed." He smiled again. "I'll deduct it from your share. Let me know when you need some more."

"Sort of puts me on the payroll," Stephen said.

"That's right. When you get back home ring up Fastline and tell 'em you got yourself another job. Which you have because there's a lot I want you to do."

Stephen felt a sense of excited relief pass through him. Things had changed. The rot had stopped even though it might only be temporary. He could use his mind again and look forward to something being accomplished. What, wasn't important.

"Stephen, there's a couple of things you've got to get really straight."

"Like what?"

"Like that wife of yours never gets close enough to get even a sniff of what's up. An' second, the story you tell her and all your mates."

"She won't care," said Stephen. "Having some money at last is all she'll bother about."

"That's at first, but once she gets used to it then the questions might start. So here's what you say." He stood up. "Come on, I'll tell you as we go back."

They walked up the path, past the pond and onto the narrow lane of overhanging trees. It was very quiet and peaceful.

He listened to Mike as he gave him his brief without interrupting. It was a bit like old times when the senior partner would sit back and explain what his contribution to the overall scheme of things was to be.

"The best way to lie is to keep as close to the truth as you can. So now you're a consultant architect working from home. Say you met up with some other blokes who've got a bit of money at the back of 'em an' a couple of nice jobs going on in the City. That means you'll be out quite a bit, no regular hours, evening meetings, that sort of thing. All of which is very nearly an actual fact. Don't ever mention my name an' don't ever ring me. I'll get in touch with you from time to time."

They were up by the car now and they could see that the tea hut had opened.

"Let's have a cuppa tea," Mike said.

They got the tea and walked out onto the graveled car park and stood talking and looking over the common.

"I got a list of things here I'll give you," Mike told him. "Reckon it'll take about ten days for you to sort it all out. Then there'll be a meeting, like a conference. You can get the original plans of the building all right, can't you?"

"Sure," said Stephen. "There won't be any problems with that. Just one thing though. You said not to mention your name. Well, when I have to meet the rest, I'd rather not have mine mentioned, you know."

"Yeah." Mike thought, then smiled. "Why not stick to your old Fastline number, eh? One-nine. I rather fancy that."

Stephen laughed. "Marvelous."

"Right, one-nine, I'll be seeing you. Oh here, I almost forgot." He handed him a single sheet of folded paper. "Don't lose it. An' here, do me a favor." He gave Stephen his empty cup and walked to the Rover.

Stephen went back into the hut and bought himself another cup of tea and a packet of biscuits. He watched the car as it moved away and out of sight.

He stopped at a flower shop in Wimbledon Village and bought a dozen roses from the money Mike had given him. It did not occur to him that the flowers were the first proceeds from an endeavor that months before he would have rejected without question.

People joked about the idea of a robbery, but there

was an attractiveness about it. Providing of course that there was no ugliness. Few would have carried the idea into fact. The relief that Stephen felt because his basic creativity was again to be released obscured any feelings of conscience he might have had.

He entered his home affected by this sudden change and with a resolve that even his marriage would improve.

"Jennifer," he called out. "Jenny, where are you?"

She was in the girls' bedroom when she heard him. She came down the openwork staircase, her blonde hair a mess, rubber gloves protecting her hands. He was standing by the door, clutching the twelve wrapped red roses.

"Good God," she said. "Who gave you those?"

"I bought them."

"Where'd you get the money? It isn't dole day, is it?"

"It's a celebration. We're back in business."

"Really, as what?"

He went through to the kitchen, put the roses in the sink and searched the cupboards for something to drink.

"I've gone into partnership," he said. "On a freelance basis." He found a half bottle of Scotch which still had enough whiskey left to make a couple of decent drinks.

"Where's the money coming from?"

"Oh, they've got money," he told her. "No problem about that. They've even given me the first month's retainer in advance." He handed her the drink. "Well, here's to the road back."

She looked puzzled but she took the drink and she raised it to him before taking a sip.

He spent the first four days writing postal orders he bought with the cash. It was amazing what even a comparatively small amount of money all at once, with the promise of more to come, could do. His appetite picked up, his temper lost its razor edge and his energy returned.

He began working again at what he knew. Studying plans, doing surveys, calculating, approximating time schedules. As the time drew near for him to meet the others and present his contribution, he began writing his presentation.

Jennifer was conscious of his activity and the difference it was making in him, but she still held back. Her sense of security had been so shattered that it was difficult for her to believe she could ever recover. She felt something had been destroyed.

Stephen was working hard until late in the evenings and she felt she had to get out of the house. So she accepted the invitation to go to a preopening rehearsal of the new play Tony was in.

She didn't ask Stephen if he wanted to go. He could stay in with the girls. She made them their supper and set the table for them before she left.

"I'm taking the car," she said. "Don't wait up. Paula may come backstage after and we'll go off and have a bite to eat or something."

"I should think even as dutiful a wife as Paula has had enough of that play by now," Stephen said.

"Then maybe Tony and I will get drunk together."

"Drive carefully," he said.

Stephen sighed and cleaned off the nib of his black drawing pen. That was it, finished. He had checked the measurements, the angles, and it was a good drawing. Not exactly like the work he had been used to, rather a different outcome envisaged. Still it had to be accurate.

His older daughter, Liz, was leaning against the door.

"How's work?" she said.

"Oh, fine." He rolled up the drawing and fed it into the long cardboard cylinder so that she would not see what it was. She had become quite expert at reading his drawings.

"What's it for?"

"A shopping precinct, in the north. Very ordinary." He hated lying to her.

She collapsed into the deep armchair and crossed her long, long legs. She put a serious, understanding look on her face. "How's it with Mummy?"

"Always questions. What do you mean?"

"Dad. Maybe Meg doesn't notice, she's only ten." Her voice sounded very superior but she could not look straight at him; she was not that confident.

"She's fine," he said.

He went on clearing the drawing table and fiddling with pens and bottles of ink. "People get frightened, you know. With change. Then they say things they don't really mean."

"I'm not getting married," she said. "Not until I'm thirty."

"That's very sensible."

She stood up, very quickly, and stretched. "Gee, I'm hungry. I'll call Meg, let's have supper, Dad. I'll pour you a beer."

The dummy bullets plowed into Connery's back. Doreen couldn't look. She hated the sight of blood even if it was phony.

She had become involved in the film and the robbery and she had imagined it was Mike because he was like the character on the screen; the leader who was tough and intelligent but who had something in him that made him care, even about the men he did not really know and had not worked with before.

They came out of the cinema and it was not yet dark.

"Let's have a stroll," Mike said.

He wants to chat about the film, she thought. They walked up King's Road and he told her the mistakes the gang had made.

"Still," he said, "in that kind of job you can't plan everything."

"You never can, can you?" she said.

"If it's the right job you can."

"They always get caught though, don't they?"

He smiled at her and they looked like two ordinary people out walking.

"I got my own little film show tomorrow," he said. "Let's have a beer."

The girls were in bed and Stephen had tested Meg on her French vocabulary. She was doing very well now, almost as well as Liz at her age.

The house was quiet and he sat with his drink thinking about his children and Jennifer and what he had gotten into. He had gone along with the tide of circumstance, clutching at a way out. At times, like now, hating himself for being carried along.

He realized that Jennifer was not the bitch she had appeared of late. There were times when he almost told her what he was doing. Perhaps if she understood just how far he was prepared to go it would be better between them.

He could have left; other men had done that. But he had stayed and that proved something, if only to himself.

It was very late when the telephone call came.

"That you, one-nine?"

"Hello. Yes, it is. Who else?"

"All ready, are you?"

"Yes."

"Right. Well get yourself over to the Lisle Private Cinema in Gerrard Street tomorrow morning at eleven."

"Eleven o'clock. Yes, I'll be there."

"One-nine, I wouldn't bring that car of yours if I was you."

There was a pause.

"I'd get a mini-cab."

The Gerrard Street district is crowded with Chinese. Old men with small, wizened faces, full of ancient wisdom and wispy beards of fine white hair; children, neat and well cared for, with mats of thick, black, straight hair and appealing, innocent round faces; the young in their tight trousers over AsiatCly slim hips, the men more attractive than the women. The community is well behaved and courteous and is the cause of very little of the trouble that occurs in the notorious Square Mile. If you want you can buy heroin in Gerrard Street.

Stephen paid the cab off in Wardour Street and walked the rest of the way. He was quickly learning the necessary caution of his new way of life. He strolled past the Shanghai Beauty Salon, the Lee Ho Fook Restaurant and the wholesale food emporium of Loon Fung. The premises he was looking for were on the opposite side of the crowded narrow street in a basement. Its neon sign was not yet blazing nor were the stills of nude girls alight in their glass display cases.

"The Lisle Private-Viewing Theatre" the sign said. "Members Only." He pushed the paint-cracked door and went into the semidarkness of a small foyer and empty paybox. The posters on the walls were full of promise: "Continuous Showing." "New Attractions." *"The Milkman's Dilemma."* There was a pair of faded curtains that hung loosely to the floor. He pushed them apart. Behind them was another door. It was locked. He pressed the white plastic button, heard its buzz and waited.

The cinema seemed very well protected and he heard the sounds of locks and bolts being sprung. At last the door was open and a tall, pale-faced man stood in the narrow opening.

"Yeah?"

"I'm one-nine."

The man inspected him and then pulled the door back so that he could go through.

"All right," he said. "Come in."

Stephen had to wait while the man snapped the locks and made the entrance secure again.

"You're the last to arrive. In here."

Stephen's eyes were accustomed to the darkness and he saw the other men fairly clearly. They were all looking at him intently. He felt uneasy and embarrassed and just nodded to them; then he sat down in the nearest of the tatty seats in the front row. He rested his briefcase on his knees and stared hard at the blank silver screen. He felt more like a dirty old man than a conspirator at a meeting of thieves.

Gardner walked across in front of the screen and went and sat beside Harry. Taylor was in the back row and on each side of him, flanking him, were two other men—Cliff and Fagan. There was no sign of Mike Daniels.

The house lights dimmed and a beam from the projection window above Taylor's head cut through the darkness to illuminate the screen. The credits of *The Milkman's Dilemma* came up but then changed to the leaders—numbers running backward from ten.

When the numbers reached zero there was a jerky cut and then a long shot of the outside of a bank building. Stephen recognized it immediately.

The bank had been filmed from the back of a car and the film image vibrated and moved with the car's motion. They were shown the bank from all available angles—from the side street up to the traffic lights with the major road junction, then all along the front, in close-up, as the car made a left turn and slowly cruised along the nearside.

Suddenly the view was changed and they were looking high up at the windows of an office building. The camera panned away and came back down and across to street level and to the bank again. The filming was not very expert because the pan was done too quickly and the scene was blurred.

Another jerky cut and they were watching inside shots of the bank. The lighting was none too good since the cameraman could only use the fixed lighting from the ceiling. It seemed to have been shot through a hole in an attaché case because the angle was low and the picture on the screen had ragged edges. There was a sense of steadied, walking movement as the cameraman went down a wide stretch of steps into an open area with a counter on one side and the large brushed-steel door of a vault on the other.

After more jerks the door opened to reveal the inside of the vault with its rows and rows of deed boxes and safes.

Harry whispered to Gardner, "Fantastic, just like *I Spy*." The pictures went black, and the white leader numbers flashed on. The house lights came up and the beam from the projection box was cut off.

After a few seconds Mike Daniels came into the viewing theatre from a door at the back.

"Right," he said. "So much for the entertainment."

He walked to the front and stood looking into the rows of seats.

Taylor's voice came out of the dimness. "Not exactly *Rififi*, was it?" He was leaning back in his seat, his legs stretched out, resting on the row in front of him.

Mike was controlled and cool. "That was the City Savings Deposit Bank."

"We know that."

"That's good, Taylor," he told him. " 'Cause that's the job."

Stephen was conscious that there was a tension between the two men, as if one were trying out the other. He sat very still and watched.

Mike went to the side of the screen and turned to Harry. "Give me a hand with these, will you?"

Harry helped him set up a folding table, two chairs, a blackboard and easel.

Mike took one of the chairs, turned it so that he could rest against its upright back and stood waiting for complete attention from his audience.

"Right. Now, everyone—the bank, the security company, the law and all the thieves in London—reckons that that is one jug you cannot blow."

Taylor's voice came out of the hollow of the back row. "They're bloody right, they are."

Stephen stared at his well-polished shoes.

Mike ignored the interruption. He was confident of what was to come; he knew he could take Taylor's predictable needling.

"That bank has got so much security in the way of alarms and unscheduled patrol visits that even I can see why nobody's had a go—yet."

He moved away from the chair and started pacing up and down in front of the table while he talked.

"On top of all, the vault door is one of Mr. Chubb's better pieces of protection. It's set in twelve inches of laminated cross-ply steel. It also has a group of combination time locks working with an isolator bolt-work mechanism. That means when Mr. Bank Manager locks up for the night the connection between the bolt-thrower handle and the bolts is broken and it stays that way until it's been set to open. You try to blow out the locks and you're in it even deeper. And just for fun, inside the vault they've put a pressure differential alarm. The second you alter the air pressure, like if you cut a hole, a little light comes up on an alarm board not a mile away in the local security center."

The men were intent and eager now, waiting for every new piece of information.

"All of which means that even if you do get past the infrared beams and radio frequency waves, you stand a very good chance of getting captured."

Taylor was coming down the outside aisle. "I don't know about you but that sounds like some very good reasons for not bothering. Unless, of course, you like the idea of doing a ten in Wandsworth."

Gardner turned to Mike. While he felt the need to back up his own man, he couldn't stop himself saying, almost quietly as if to lessen the criticism, "The way you're putting it, Mike, it does sound a bit dodgy."

Mike laughed at them and his voice was full of confidence. "Dodgy? This is going to be the biggest job ever pulled. Bigger than the Train. They figure they're watertight. Well, they ain't. It's goin' to be done, an' we're goin' to do it." He paused. "There's a loophole. I could pull any one of seven banks right now, except this one's carrying four million."

There was a silence as the words were taken and digested. Stephen turned in his seat and studied the faces of the men in the cinema. He was surprised. Although he knew it was illogical he almost expected that there would be some peculiar kind of common physical denominator. Like the old wives' tale that you could always tell a murderer by his eyes. But there was none. No one looked particularly tough or sly or suspicious. They were all quietly well dressed in dark sports jackets or suits; but excepting Daniels, only Taylor had any style. He was wearing an open-necked shirt and casual, lightweight jeans and sneakers. He was tanned, well built and good-looking—he could have been an actor or a musician. There was one common factor: no one looked over thirty. He was the oldest man in the room.

"That sounds all very well, Mike, but how?" Taylor was standing at the far end of the front row, hands on his hips, legs apart.

The question cut into their excitement and reminded them that all was not quite settled or agreed. The taut attention returned and they waited.

Mike Daniels folded his arms and let his eyes travel from Stephen, to the two men at the back, to Gardner and Harry, and finally to rest on Taylor. His voice was as low, assured and dramatic as the hero in a play who has a stunning curtain line to deliver.

"We go underground. Through the sewers."

"What?" Harry wriggled in his seat. "I don't get it."

"You may not know it, but some nut wants to open the sewers to tourists, like they do in Paris. Well, I got news for 'em. I just organized the first package tour."

The atmosphere changed again and Mike knew he had done it his way. He looked down at Stephen and smiled. "Come on, it's your turn."

He sat there for a second, took a deep breath and then

clutching his briefcase stood up and walked over to the table. They watched every indecisive move he made.

"Ah, good morning, gentlemen."

"What the bloody hell's this?" said Taylor.

Oh, my God, thought Stephen. Mike was by his side as if he knew he would need the support.

"Call him one-nine, that's all you have to know. We need him and I say he's all right, so sit down and listen."

Taylor gave way and Mike moved the chairs to give Stephen more room. Then he too sat down.

Suddenly he was calm and his fingers, as they pinned the plans and papers to the blackboard, were sure and professional.

The nervousness he felt was the normal apprehension of addressing any group or sales meeting. There was an idea to sell.

He cleared his throat. "The plan, here, shows the ground and lower levels of the bank building together with the foundations and footings. The structure is prewar and fortunately survived the blitz."

He looked out at his audience with the sightless eyes of the lecturer. "It's rather a nice building, actually."

Now beginning his stride, he returned to the plan.

"The vault is located fifteen feet below ground level and rests on the reinforced concrete foundations. These are two feet thick and beneath them runs a nine-inch layer of hardcore. In turn this rests on a series of two feet six-inch footings. You can see them here, rather like blunt pegs set into the ground."

The men moved forward over the rows of seats like voyeurs at a stripshow, fascinated by the technical presentation, eager to know more.

"Fortunately for us the vault is due for upgrading. As you no doubt know, this means they will construct an inner sleeve of twelve-inch steel. At the moment the flooring is concrete reinforced with three-quarter-inch cross-laid steel bars. Now, to the sewer system. This is divided between the Greater London Council and the local borough councils, in our case the City of London. Generally speaking, the G.L.C. sewers, all seven hundred miles of them, are the largest. For example, you could drive a truck along the one under Sloane Street, if you could get it down there of course."

Mike Daniels felt very comfortable and pleased. He thought Stephen was doing marvelously, the men were hanging on every word; they were in—he knew the signs. And although he had heard it all before, he enjoyed listening.

"However, not to go into too much detail, the ones that concern us are the Northern Low Level Outfall and one of the main sewers it intercepts. The intercepting sewer, again quite adequate in size for our purposes, runs within fifteen feet of the base of the bank building vault. It is approximately twenty feet below ground level. You can see quite clearly therefore that it is perfectly feasible to tunnel out and up from this sewer to a point directly beneath the interior of the vault."

He turned from the blackboard and looked down at Mike, getting the smile of approval he no longer needed.

"Thus, we have established our mode of entry and subsequent escape. The exact dimensions and measurements have, incidentally, been rigorously checked out. The work party will be divided into two groups. The suggestion is"—he consulted the papers on the table—"Cliff and Gardner above ground level. Their function being the vitally important one of communication."

The two men, at the mention of their names, reacted self-consciously and Gardner glanced back to the row behind him to acknowledge Cliff. He's not much more than a boy, he thought. Hope he knows his bleeding way around. Could do with a haircut too.

"The remainder of us, Mike Daniels, Taylor, ahmm, Fagan?" He looked up from the table to confirm that he had got the name of Taylor's second man right. The man gave him a studied nod of recognition with a head that was bald except for a few carefully brushed black strands of hair. "Yes, Fagan and then Harry, and, of course, myself. All of us below ground. It is obviously essential that each member be fully aware not only of his own duties but those of his associates. Mike, naturally, is in overall command of the operation with specific responsibility for the method of entry through the vault floor. Taylor, one might say, has executive status and is in charge of the technical preparations, the underground work plan and the general discipline during training. Fagan, Harry and myself will be allocated an individual, detailed duty program. No doubt you will have gathered that beyond my own involvement as a working member I have, ahmm, a technical advisory capacity.

"That, gentlemen, in broad outline, is the basic plan. I believe you will find that we have catered for a considerable permutation of possible eventuality. In short it is my view that the enterprise has a very high success potential."

They were stunned—not only by what they had been told, but by the very proper and businesslike delivery.

"Brother," said Taylor "I think maybe you're all right."

Stephen sat down smiling at the compliment, masking his enjoyment by shuffling and collecting the plans and papers from the table.

"Any questions?" Mike was standing now, tall and sure of himself.

"Well," said Taylor. "You're right, it sounds great. But what about that alarm? You say it'll go the second we're in through the vault."

"That's the loophole. It does go. But we're inside, aren't we? So what happens?"

"I'll tell you," said Fagan. "Two carloads of old Bill, the keyholder and the security mob descend on the bloody lot of us." His voice was thick with an East End Jewish slur.

"Right," said Mike. "But we're in the one place they can't get. They can trample all over the manor if they want. But nobody, not even the vault maker, can get into that vault until the time lock operates. And by then, mate, we'll be under the hill and far away."

Stephen felt confident enough to interrupt with his own observation. "Like most brilliant ideas, it's really quite simple."

"But we're goin' to need a load of gear down there, ain't we?" Harry looked around at the others, glad he had something to say but hoping it didn't sound too much like an objection.

"Don't worry, that'll be taken care of." Mike turned to Taylor. "You still got that place in the country?"

"You mean the flying business? Yeah, it's still a goer."

"Okay, I want it fixed so that we can all move in, we'll live there, train and rehearse. Any problem?"

"You can have it in twenty-four hours. Okay?"

Mike smiled at him. "I thought you might say that."

Gardner's long, pale face looked up at them. "Just one thing. What if the law suspects we're down there?"

"Psychology. Remember it'll be the uniformed boys who'll show up. This has never been done before so they got no modus operandi to go on. They can see there's no one in the place and no sign of an entry. So, they'll reckon there's a fault in the alarm. It happens often enough."

The arrangements were made, the questions answered, they were convinced. Stephen waited behind as the rest of them left the cinema, one by one at intervals of five minutes.

"What did you think of them?" Mike asked.

"I'm not sure. Surprised, I suppose. I thought they would be more, well, sinister and a lot older. They're so young."

Mike laughed at him. "Expect a load of ancient lags in Cagney gear, did you? I tell you the youth has come to crime just like everything else."

With the house lights up the little cinema looked sad, an old flea pit that had seen better days.

"You been watching too many lousy films where all the villains have scars and talk out the side of their mouths. All nice and cut and dried."

Stephen laughed. "Yes, you're right, I guess. Brought up on B pictures and television."

"Yeah. Well, they're not idiots, not even Fagan."

"What are they then?"

"Thieves. You might just as well say salesmen or clerks in an office. It's their business. It's what they do. There's nothing strange about it, not to them anyway. If anything's strange it's you. Sweating away for a lifetime of what? Being taken, that's what you are, all over the place, only it's called business."

"People don't get hurt that way, Mike."

"Don't they? What about the poor bastards whose savings get sold up the river 'cause one of your nice, respectable businessmen does a little deal on the side?"

"They can't be thieves all the time. What else do they do?"

"Jesus, what do you expect? They do what everybody

does. They have girl friends or wives and children and hobbies. They build shelves in the kitchen and clean their cars on Sundays. There's nothing else you have to know. Nobody goes talking or looking into people on this sort of job. You choose 'em and they do a job and that's it. After that it's all over and maybe you see 'em again, maybe you don't. What they are isn't important or what they're really like, there's no bleeding personnel officer here. Can they do something or can't they? Will they or won't they? That lot can and now they will. Simple. Forget the rest, you don't have to know 'em or even like 'em. Just learn to work with them, that's all."

Stephen walked ahead of Mike as they went out into the street.

"I won't offer you a lift," Mike said.

"No, that's all right, I think I'll take the bus anyway."

"You'd better tell that wife of yours you're going to be away for a spell."

"Zip me up, will you?" He held the material in his left hand and pulled the zipper, watching her skin being closed off as the teeth clenched. "There's a hook at the top." He found it and slid it into the loop of thick cotton. He wanted to touch and hold her shoulders but he knew that would annoy her, as if touching the finished product would somehow damage it.

"There," she said, "I'm ready."

Stephen turned away and looked at himself in the

long mirror that hung on the inside of the louvered wardrobe. He had been out of doors a lot, traveling and organizing, and the sun had burned away the sallowness in his face.

"You should buy a lamp," Jennifer said. "You always look so much better with a tan."

He talked back to her reflection in the mirror. "You look very good."

She clipped the gold charm bracelet around her left wrist and then started checking the contents of her small evening handbag.

She was wearing long, black silk culottes and a white top that looked like a Russian shirt. The neck was open and she had tied a silk scarf under the collar and into a loose knot so that her throat was bare.

"Shall we go?" she said.

The evenings were still very warm and he had booked an outside table at San Lorenzo, an Italian restaurant facing onto Wimbledon High Street, whose entrance was at the back in a mews. There was a paved path with plants along one side and a sand pit with overhanging trees on the other. The Italians who ran the restaurant had a reputation for encouraging patrons to bring their children, and it had become a very chic place for families to have lunch on Saturdays. The waiters wore wide-bottomed casual trousers and colored shirts and were very friendly and hospitable.

"They've beaten us to it," Stephen said.

Jennifer could see Tony and Paula sitting at a table

by the edge of the sand pit. Tony saw them come in and stood up. He put his arms round Jennifer and kissed her on the cheek. "Sexiest mother south of the river."

Stephen went to the table and kissed Paula once on either cheek breathing in her perfume, just for an instant enjoying the physical contact with another woman.

"We took the liberty of having a drink while we waited," said Tony. "Actually we're quite pissed." He had his arm stretched along the back of Jennifer's chair. She enjoyed his outward, easy charm.

They talked and laughed the way friends do who have known each other for a long time but take care not to get too close in case they run out of gossip and are left only with themselves.

"The brandies are on me," said Tony.

"Don't be bloody silly," Stephen told him. "This is our evening."

"I'm going to insist, mate," he said. He moved closer to Jennifer. "Let's all get blind and have an orgy."

Paula laughed but it was necessary for her to make the effort. She could never be sure with Tony. She guessed there had been other women: you can't spend weeks on end living through rehearsals and out-of-town openings without becoming involved. It was human nature, she thought. So she moved nearer to Stephen and played the game.

"How are you doing now, Stephen? Jenny said something about free-lance consultant."

"Yes," he said. "It's with a small group."

"Is it better than being with a company?"

"It's better than what I was doing. Almost anything is better than that."

She, almost involuntarily, put her hand over his as it lay on the white of the table cloth. "Will it work for you?"

Stephen thought it was the nose that saved her face from being chocolate box pretty. Her dark hair was long and loose and full, her skin smooth olive and her dark eyes deep and warm. The nose had a bump in it, it gave her character.

"I hope so," he said. "There's a good chance it might."

Tony looked across the table at him. "I hear you're going away for a couple of weeks, Stephen."

"That's right. There's a development up north, offices, shops, flats."

"We'll have to take care of Jenny while you're gone. Have our own little development." Tony laughed at Jennifer and squeezed her arm.

"You're wicked," she said.

"Ah, but you love it."

Stephen felt his possessiveness rise up as he looked at his wife. Maybe it would do them both good if she had an affair, and he did too.

"What's the play about?" Stephen said. "Jennifer hasn't told me."

Tony took his arm away from Jennifer and for the

first time during the evening became serious. He leaned over the table and Stephen thought it was very funny that the flirting stopped as soon as Tony was to talk about himself.

"There's a double layer plot going on because the character I play spends the first act wrestling with his conscience. He works out all the motives so that for him they fit nice and neatly, only from where the audience sits it's all twisted. You know, you make your justifications and end up calling them principles. So he convinces himself that what he plans to do is right. Then he does it."

"That was too complicated for me," said Jennifer.

Stephen sipped his brandy and it was not only because it was brandy that he held the glass tightly cupped in the palms of his hands.

"Does he get away with it?"

The answer was suddenly very necessary to him.

Tony laughed. "Oh, come on. You don't want me to spoil it for you."

"I want to know."

"Well, if it's that important." The atmosphere had lost the fun Tony had generated. "No, he doesn't." He tried to recapture the light tone. "We can't have the customers thinking crime pays, can we?"

"That's nonsense," Stephen said. "It pays all the time. You think big business is straight? We'd all be at it, only most of us are too damned scared of getting caught."

"I don't think that's right," Tony said and his voice

was low and without humor. "I think most people are honest."

"I don't suppose you two have got any time for a holiday this year, have you?" Jennifer said.

They drove home in the special kind of boiling silence that only married couples can create. Stephen deliberately drove fast and used the low gears to take the corners at speed so that Jennifer had to hold onto the dashboard.

When they got back to the house they went up to see the girls.

Finally they got into bed with exaggerated care, so that they did not touch each other. She pulled the sheets over her shoulders and turned away from him. He reached for the packet of cigarettes on his bedside table, and as he blew the first stream of smoke into the bedroom air, she turned and with a twisted face asked him if he would mind not smoking. It was his cue to throw the bedclothes back, get into his dressing gown and go downstairs to the sitting room to smoke and to glower to himself about her infuriating stupidity.

She lay in bed knowing that they were both playing out a marriage game. It was necessary for her to provoke him even if it meant making herself a bitch. They had to reestablish their relationship, their realness together. She loved him and she wanted him but he had to regain his self-respect. When he had that, she could respect him again and it would bring them together.

3

The orange wind sock was battered into a limp rag by the downpour of rain. The furrows in the grass runway made by the light single-fan planes when they landed were soggy with mud. There was no one about—no lights or signs of life in the clubhouse or radio control room.

Mike Daniels parked the Rover outside the vast corrugated metal hangar, switched off the engine and then sounded the horn.

Less than a minute later a door in the retractable side of the hangar opened. Taylor stood in the doorway hunched against the rain. Mike made a dash from the car to the hangar and when he was in, Taylor locked the door behind them. They stood together like two factory inspectors and watched the men as they worked.

In the center of the floor there was a large van. To the side of it a skirt had been added so that you could not see the under part of it. Cliff sat perched on the tailboard and inside Gardner was working at an overhead gantry that had been built into the reinforced roof.

Laid out on the floor of the hangar in neat groups were sets of equipment.

The two men walked to the wall and Taylor took a clipboard that was hanging there.

"How are you doing, Mike?" Cliff called out and the other men looked up briefly from their work. They were intent, involved and conscious of being part of a team, each member relying on the contribution of the others.

"Five sets of sewermen's gear complete. Safety apparatus, lamps, manila hand lines."

They moved along the line.

"Lifting harness, first-aid kits. Sets of compressed air, breathing apparatus with cylinders. Nine Spiralarm gas detection lamps. Lead acetate papers in airtight packs and wire cages.

"Now over here, your cutting equipment, cylinders of oxygen, rods, blowtorch, two sets of cutters, chisels, picks, shovels and miscellaneous digging equipment. Specially constructed collapsible plastic trolleys. Plastic food containers and vacuum flasks. And, a prefabricated pontoon. Rather proud of that, I am."

"It looks great, Taylor," Mike told him. "How's the shoring coming along?"

"All right," he said. "Let's have a look at the van."

They moved away from the lines of equipment and climbed into the back of the van. "Watch that hole."

In the center of the floor of the van a circular hole had been cut and rimmed with rubber. Mike looked into the hole and saw that a narrow shaft had been dug into the ground directly under it.

"Do you want a demonstration?" Gardner asked them. Taylor nodded. "Okay, then, just give me a hand with the cylinder."

They helped him lift a cylinder of oxygen which they attached to the chains that hung from the overhead gantry.

When it was in position Gardner called out to Cliff, "All ready to go?" Outside Cliff had put a heavy-duty jack under the front axle of the van and started to jack it up. His young arms flexed with the exertion and the heart and arrow tattoo on his right forearm seemed to beat with its own rhythm. As the angle of the van altered, the cylinder on the gantry started to move along the steel guide lines toward the back doors.

"Hold it steady, Taylor, don't want it swinging around."

Taylor held the cylinder until it reached the end of the gantry run which put the cylinder directly over the hole in the floor of the van.

"Right now, down we go."

Gardner carefully drew the chain pulley, hand over hand, and the cylinder slowly disappeared through the hole. Mike leaned over and watched it as it entered the shaft under the van; when it reached the bottom, which was not very deep, it stopped.

"There," Gardner said. "That gives you an idea, don't it?"

"How long to unload the lot?" said Mike.

"About fifteen minutes, I should say. There'll be five of you in here on the big day, won't there?"

Taylor smiled at Mike. He was very pleased with the way it had gone. He knew the need for organization and timing and he was proud of the way he had brought the men and the equipment together and made them work.

"You and Cliff been over your part of it?" Mike asked.

"Yeah, we're going through it all the time. There shouldn't be no problems."

"No," said Mike. "Let's hope not."

"You don't have to worry," Taylor said.

"I'm not. Let's see how one-nine's getting along."

As they left, Cliff started lowering the front of the van and inside Gardner pulled the cylinder out of the hole. They would go through the actions many times again because they wanted to be very sure that the van jacked up to just the right angle. Too high and the cylinder would race along the track and crash through the closed back doors of the van, which would not be the best thing to happen on a busy city street in broad daylight.

In a corner of the hangar, working quietly on their own, Stephen, Harry and Fagan were adjusting and testing the prefabricated aluminum shoring equipment that Stephen had designed. The two men did not interrupt them but stood and watched.

The unit looked like the letter H with the crossbar of the letter broken in the middle to form an upright V. Underneath the V they had placed a hand hydraulic jack. Stephen was pumping the jack and as it lengthened, it pushed the center of the V into a horizontal position; this in turn widened the top part of the uprights until the letter was misshapen.

"Will it work?"

Stephen turned round and saw Mike and Taylor watching.

"Hello," he said. "Of course it will work. We've dug out a small tunnel at the back. Tomorrow we'll run a test under actual operating conditions."

"What about those uprights?" Taylor said.

Stephen stood up and with his hands demonstrated for them.

"You have to imagine the structure in situ. The uprights are pressing into the side of the tunnel, so as the center bar rises they settle into the hard clay and take up the tension. We place aluminum sheets along the top of the horizontal bar between each unit. It won't give a great deal of room to maneuver, but then we don't need very much at that point. Once underneath the vault floor, the foundations of the building will supply their own support."

Mike laughed. "Very good, one-nine."

"Yes," he said, "I thought you'd like it."

"That's about it, Mike," Taylor said. "There's just a few more things to get together and we're all ready to go."

The men stood looking at Mike and he knew that they were waiting for him to give them some indication of when.

"It won't be long now," he said. "I'll be letting you know. Don't worry."

Taylor walked with him to the door in the side of the hangar. When he opened it, the rain blew onto them.

93

"It shouldn't be too long," he said. "They'll get edgy if they have to hang about."

"I know," said Mike. "We just have to wait on the weather."

"Just how tricky is it down there?"

"Depends on how careful you are."

"I hear sewermen don't go down if it's raining."

"That's right. A storm like this could fill a nine-foot sewer in very much of a hurry."

"Christ," said Taylor.

"So wait and keep checking with the weather bureau."

Mike walked through the rain to the Rover. Taylor went with him and stood by the open window of the driving door. Mike looked up at him as he revved the engine.

"No problem about closing this place, was there?"

Taylor's eyes glanced at the sign swinging from the veranda of the clubhouse, "Taylor's Aero Club."

"No," he said. "I just wrote and told all the members we was closed for renovations."

"Good. I've been thinking it might be an idea if you were to give some of 'em a little bit of relaxation time. Have some yourself."

"A rest wouldn't go amiss."

"Leave Harry and Cliff to keep a watch out."

"All right," said Taylor.

Mike put the car into gear and as it started to move away he nodded to Taylor. "I'll let you know the time."

The car bumped across the grass runway onto the

asphalt roadway that led to the country lane toward the village that was seven miles from the small airfield.

Taylor stood in the rain and watched the car until it was out of sight. His fair hair was tightening into close curls on his head. It always did that when it got wet.

Mike Daniels was enjoying himself as he swung the small boat around the twists and turns of the river. He was a city man but the country still held a visiting magic, especially in good weather. He had dressed for the occasion in sneakers, blue boating jeans and a white-and blue-striped sweat shirt. He hadn't gone all the way and bought a skipper's cap, but in the cabin he had a boating sweater, just in case the weather turned.

Doreen had packed a very good picnic for him and Stephen and he had bought cans of beer which he put into a plastic sack and hung by a length of thick string over the side of the boat so that they would be pulled through the cool water. He never could drink warm beer.

He steered the boat through a part of the water where the trees had been ripped away from the bank. Farther up nature took over again and the scene became what you would expect in that part of the country.

Stephen was a real fisherman and he was used to walking over long tracts of land to find the right spot on a river to fish. He liked to be alone so that he could forget about everything else and immerse himself in the business of ground bait and tackle. Because he had become a dry-fly trout fisherman he did not hold course fishing in the same regard anymore.

He knew that this part of the Thames did not have trout so he decided to settle for a few roach and perhaps a perch.

He heard the chugging of an old engine before he saw a motorboat turn into his stretch of water. There had been very few boats up that far and he guessed that it was probably Mike.

Taylor had told Stephen that since they were all ready they could take some time off, provided they kept out of trouble and near a telephone. Mike had got a message to Stephen that he would like to have a talk, and meeting on the river had been Stephen's idea: it gave him a chance to mix business with pleasure, and in any case he thought it was a good place for it.

Mike cut the engine and let the boat drift toward the bank.

That's ruined it for a few hours, Stephen thought, as he reeled in his line.

"Caught anything?"

Stephen tipped up his keep net and let the two small roach gently back into the river. "I was doing all right," he said.

"Give me a hand, will you."

Mike threw the mooring rope onto the bank and

Stephen tied it to the thick trunk of an overhanging tree. Then he held the rope taut so that Mike could climb out of the boat with the picnic basket.

"Keep hold," he said and pulled up the bag with the beer. He jumped onto the bank, took two cans of beer and then let the bag back into the water and tied its string onto the mooring line.

Stephen stood and watched him as he ripped open the metal seals which popped and spurted out streams of beer froth.

"Here," he said, handing one to Stephen.

"That's better," Mike said. He sat down on the bank and opened the lid of the basket. "How about a little food?"

"I'll give you a hand," Stephen said.

Between them they spread out a cloth, paper plates, knives and forks. Doreen had packed the sandwiches in tin foil and put them into white plastic boxes to keep them fresh.

"Now what have we got here? Tomato and cheese, ham and pickle, some banana, a couple of pork pies and some crisps. Done us proud, she has."

"Haven't got any salt, have you?" Stephen asked.

"She'll have put it on," Mike said.

The men ate their lunch silently. Stephen tried to start a conversation between sandwiches but Mike was not used to talking with his meals.

When they finished their lunch Mike drew the bag from the river and opened two more beers. Then he lay back in the sun and blew the smoke from his cigarette up through the branches of the trees.

"Bloody marvelous here, isn't it?" he said.

"Yes, it is. I don't know why we bother to live in a town."

"Excitement," Mike said. "All right for a visit but I couldn't live out here. I mean, what do you do when it rains? Sit and stare at it?"

There was a plop, like the sound of a stone hitting the water. Mike jerked upright. "What was that?"

Stephen laughed at him. "It's the dace jumping in the water. They're having a game."

The cigarette stub made an arc in the air and landed in the water with a hiss. "Tell me, how's everything been at the club, one-nine?"

"Very good. Everything's ready."

"No problems?"

"None. Taylor would make a great executive, you know."

"Yeah, that's one reason why I picked him."

"No, I don't mean for this, I mean in a job. He'd be very good."

"You're a funny bugger, you know that. What makes you think any of us want that? What's so wonderful about being straight?"

They looked at each other across the tablecloth, like two men setting up for a debate.

"Because up until now that's all I've known—it's my standard. It was how I was brought up, to work for a living, to contribute."

"You're talking like a prison reformer. I've been in front of them, you know, and every time I tell 'em don't go giving me that broken-home chat. Hundreds of blokes come from a broken home but they're not all thieves, are they?"

"Why do you do it then?" Stephen leaned over and took a cigarette from the pack that Mike had left on the grass.

"I like the money. It's as simple as that. There's nothing else I could do that would pay as well."

"How do you equate it with the risk? Do you say to yourself, well, if I steal so much and get caught then it works out at such and such a year?"

Mike laughed at him. "You can't understand, can you? Listen, if I had ten grand in my place and the law came to turn me over I'd give it all back to stay clean; 'an you just can't think that way. If every time I was going out to do a post office or something and I was thinking, well, if I get captured then there's seven years up the spout for a few grand, I'd never go out. But of course this job is different."

Stephen tapped the ash from his cigarette into the water and watched as it drifted away on the slow swell of the tide.

"Yes," he said and there was pride in his voice. "This is rather big, isn't it?"

"It's not that," said Mike. "I know that if I did get caught on this one it would be different, because of what I tried to do. It's not the money. Having done it makes me different. I could have been an insignificant little petty thief before, getting three months here and three months there. But if I was up at the Old Bailey an' old Bill had the needle to me, I could be in a lot of trouble. The judge would say that I thought it up, and he could hand out twenty years. I might have only nicked a pound but it's the way I did it, the enormity of it."

"Then why are you going to do it?"

"It's the challenge, I think. It's never been done before, has it?" He smiled. "But I'm not doing it by thinking about the nick. It's like I told you: we can't get caught. We might not get any money, but we won't get caught."

"I think I'll have another beer if you've got one," Stephen said.

"Help yourself, an' I'll have one while you're at it."

Stephen pulled the bag up and took out the last two cans.

"What about you, then?" Mike asked. "You're not going to tell me that being up to your bleedin' neck in debt has suddenly turned you to a life of crime?"

"I don't suppose I actually know. For someone like me it's one way out. I was so far down that it didn't matter anymore. Not working destroys you. It's being one of the famous middle classes. You have all the pride but none of the guts. If I were on my own it would be different. I could just go away and start again. You can't do that with a wife and two children."

In some ways he is quite pathetic, Mike thought; but he said, "You could if you wanted to enough."

"Perhaps I don't want to then." He took another cigarette from the packet. "I don't know. Money ruins people. Particularly when you haven't got it. All you think about is that having it would solve everything. And it would of course. For a time anyway." He came out of his reverie and smiled. "So here I am, an arch criminal."

"You're here because you want to be, mate," Mike said. "I don't know what makes a thief, I don't think anyone knows. But it's a bloody sight better than being hard up."

"Maybe we're all thieves," Stephen said. "Maybe we'd all like to do just one big job. Look how everybody was sorry when they caught the train robbers. It's a kind of Robin Hood permissive socialism."

"How's your swimming?"

"Not bad," said Stephen. "But not good enough."

"You know, don't you?"

They stood on the grass bank, serious again.

"About the rain? Yes, I know. Let's hope it keeps fine for us."

"Yeah," said Mike. "But this is England, mate, and that's something you can't guarantee. No matter how many times you check with the weather bureau."

"I thought you were sure about everything."

"I'm just being bloody realistic, that's all," Mike said.

"If you told the others they might not feel too keen about coming along."

"Taylor has an idea," Mike said. "But you got to remember something called greed. That's what gets 'em all. They know there's a few million quid to be had and they're all set to take it. A little drop of rain ain't going to put 'em off now, believe me."

They packed up and Stephen took his rod apart. He held the rope again so that Mike could climb into the boat.

Mike picked up the starting handle and put it into position. The motor sparked into life on the second swing.

"You'd better stay close to home," he said. "I think we're in for a fine spell."

Stephen threw him the rope and put his foot against the prow of the boat, pushing it free from the mud bottom. The boat drifted in the current and moved slowly out into the middle of the river.

The flat was on the fifth floor of a building in Chelsea. It had little to distinguish it from any other flat in the block. The rooms were spaced as if a child had solved a simple geometrical problem with open cubes. You got the footage you paid for.

A small hall led to a sitting room off of which was a tiny kitchen. Leading from the hall was the bedroom and minute bathroom. It would not need much imagination to deduce that it was a bachelor's flat. The only books and magazines in the place were devoted to sports, body building and naked girls.

A small table lamp had been left burning in the sitting room, but the rest was in darkness. Sounds of the night drifted up to the fifth floor and mixed with the sound of two people making love.

Grunts and sighs were suddenly cut off by the shrill ringing of the bedside telephone.

"Bloody marvelous." The voice was Taylor's.

He stretched his arm across the bed and found the receiver.

"Yeah?"

Abruptly his mood changed and he sat up in the bed and switched on the single bedside lamp.

"Yeah, I got it," he said. "Okay."

Very carefully he put the receiver back onto its cradle. The girl beside him leaned on one elbow and smiled at him because she did not want his mood to change.

"Who was that?"

Taylor, suddenly remembering that she was there, turned and said, "The weatherman."

The girl tried to laugh, but she did not make a very convincing job of it. "Very comical," she said. Taylor ignored her warm naked body and walked into the bathroom. The girl could hear the sound of the shower and she followed Taylor into the bathroom.

He was standing under the water, bracing himself against the high-speed needle spray. The girl was about to join him, but as the water touched her she screamed and jumped back.

"You must be mad. A cold shower?"

Taylor yelled at her through the water, "I'm in training baby. It'll have to wait."

Jennifer was in the kitchen clearing away their supper and when the telephone rang there was no point in him trying to get to it before her. He waited. She came into the room and there was a look of deliberate interest on her face.

"That was your new boss."

"What do you mean was?" he said.

"Oh, he trusted me with the message," she told him.

Stephen got up from the chair and turned down the volume on the television set. "What did he say?"

"He sounds rather nice. Rough but attractive. Is he attractive?"

"Yes," said Stephen. "He's a real Steve McQueen. What did he say?"

"He said the meeting's on for tomorrow. He'll expect you at ten."

"I see."

"Is it important?"

He looked straight into her eyes—something he had not done for quite a long time.

"Yes," he said. "It is very important. I'll be away for maybe a couple of days."

"Oh, and what then?"

"Then everything should be all right," he said.

"I think I'll go up," she said. "Do you want a coffee?"

"Yes," he said. "I want to see the end of the program."

She went back into the kitchen, made him his coffee and took it into the sitting room.

"Here you are. You shouldn't stay up too late, not with that meeting in the morning."

"No, I won't," he said and took the coffee from her without letting his eyes leave the screen.

"Good night then," she said.

"I won't be long."

The bathwater was very hot and soothing. She had put some scented oil into the water and she lay there enjoying the sensual feeling the heavy water gave her body. She got out of the bath before the water had cooled, and wrapped herself in a large bathtowel and sat on the edge of the bath. She did not rub herself dry but just dabbed the sweat from her face. When most of the water had evaporated she went into their bedroom and sat at her make-up table and made a close inspection of her face.

The lines around her eyes were beginning to show—not very surprising, she thought, considering what I've been through. She had sensed that there was something more than just normally important about the telephone call from Stephen's boss. Stephen had changed since he had got tied up with the new people. He had lost that awful cringing look she hated.

She took a packet of eye pads from the drawer in the make-up table and went and lay down on the bed and put a pad on each eye. They were cool and refreshing and she relaxed on the bed.

The program was over and Stephen switched off the television. As he went around the ground floor putting off lights and locking up for the night, he found that he felt intoxicated. He was conscious of his body and the way it moved and operated as if he had suddenly become strong. Maybe he had absorbed some of the strength of the actors in the TV series.

In the bathroom he felt the sweet humidity of Jennifer's bath. He washed and cleaned his teeth, changed into his pajamas and left his day clothes neatly folded on the wicker bathroom chair. Then he went into the bedroom.

She was still lying there with the pads on her eyes and she did not hear him come in. The towel had slipped and Stephen could see her breasts and brown, firm nipples. Her long legs were folded one over the other and the light brown hair had dried thick and fluffy from the bath. He stood by the side of the bed looking down at her and for the first time in months he felt himself rise and go hard.

He leaned over and kissed her between her legs. Her legs opened and then her arms were around him and her hands were feeling him. He was strong and rough with her and she reacted. It was as if they were fighting together, fighting away the aggression, the pent up emotions and tension that had built up over their bad times.

When it was over they drew up the bedclothes and

went to sleep, her body pressing close to his back, her arm stretched over his thighs and her hand holding him as they drifted off into the first gentle, relaxed sleep their marriage had given them since their troubles began.

The dark summer night was warm and still, there were no lights that any passerby could see around the Aero Club or the hangar.

Harry and Cliff sat playing cards at a table that was littered with empty, dirty plates. One ashtray was filled with burnt cigarette stubs. They had helped themselves to the liquor cupboard and a half-empty bottle of gin and some used bottles of tonic water were on another table.

They were playing five-card stud, what they would call a friendly game. That meant they kept the betting down to pennies. Also they knew this was the last night they would spend together at the hangar and they were being careful to keep the atmosphere between them cool since the next day would be the start of what brought them together.

Finally they threw their cards in and Harry pulled the pot of money over to his side of the table and started to count it.

"Reckon that just about evens it up," he said. "How about a turn round the grounds?"

They stood outside the clubhouse waiting to get accustomed to the dark. Then they walked over to the radio control room and checked the door. It was locked firm.

"You won't get anybody out here at this time of night," Harry said.

"Can't tell," said Cliff.

They went toward the hangar.

"You ever been down a sewer?" said Harry.

"No."

"It's the rats I don't fancy."

"They're no bother," said Cliff. "It's the turds you got to watch out for."

"Oh, very charmin'," said Harry. "That's just what I bleedin' need, a boot full of shit."

"Mike says it's as healthy as any other job. The rainwater washes it away. You told your missus about this one?"

They had reached the hangar and Cliff tried the lock on the door that was inset into the corrugated end of the hangar.

That was firm too.

"I wouldn't tell her anything," said Harry. "She couldn't hold her tongue."

Mike Daniels sipped the hot chocolate Doreen had made for him and went over the marks and measurements on the plans. Every now and then he would stop and think and then go on.

He heard Doreen come into the kitchen and for an instant he thought of covering over the papers, like a boy does at school when he doesn't want anyone to look over his shoulder. But he didn't bother. She was in her quilted dressing gown and she went to the gas stove to make herself a hot drink.

"You done all your calls?"

"What, oh yeah."

"I've got a nice bit of cake. Have a piece of cake, Mike. It'll do you good."

"No thanks, love."

She poured the hot milk into the mug, added the sugar and the chocolate powder and sat down opposite her husband. She could not bring herself to read the papers and they both knew that.

"I'm going to be away, you know," he said.

"Yeah. I thought you would. How long this time?"

"It depends," he said. He seemed about to explain it to her but she interrupted him.

"Don't tell me, Mike. I don't want to know."

"You like what it gets you though, don't you?"

"Course I do," she said. "But that don't mean I gotta know. It's bad enough as it is."

"Well, after this there might not be any more."

She stirred her mug and then drank some of the chocolate.

"I'll believe that when it happens."

"I mean it," he said.

She looked across the table at him and her face was

tired—from looking after a man and two children and from the worry, most of all from the worry.

"It won't do us no good, you know. I mean it won't do no good if you have to go an' . . ."

"Don't worry," he said. He stretched his hand across the table and patted her arm.

She held back the tears—something she had learned to do—and had another sip of her hot chocolate.

"It must be big then?"

"A bit," he said.

"You gonna be all right? How long before I know?"

"Not long. Just stay near the flat. I'll let you know."

He folded up the plans and the papers and very carefully filed the papers into a black plastic envelope.

"I'll tell you this now," he said. "So you'll have time. I thought about this a lot, I mean it's not just a last-minute thing."

She sat very still with her hands clasped around the mug; she had the look of a woman who fears what is to come. So he smiled at her. "Now come, gel, it's nothing like that."

Her face relaxed a little and she felt more at ease.

"If everything goes all right, you know. Then I think that maybe it was time we got out and saw something. There's a place I've been looking over, from books and things. Seems very nice. Good schools, lovely weather, great."

"My God," she said. "This is it, isn't it? It's what you been on about, it's that big."

He couldn't help the look of pride he knew she could see on his face.

"Yeah, could be. Anyway get prepared, just in case."

"What about you?" she said. "You gonna be all right?"

"Don't worry, I know how to take care, don't I?"

"I'll wait then," she said.

At exactly eight minutes past ten on a sunny Friday morning a newly painted green van came out of the Knightsbridge Underpass into Piccadilly and filtered into the stream of traffic that was heading east toward the center of the West End of London.

The van was being driven by Cliff, wearing workman's overalls, and by his side, in the passenger seat, sat Gardner similarly dressed, watching the stream of traffic. Occasionally he looked at his watch.

Inside the van five men sat in tight spaces between cylinders, prefabricated building units, lighting equipment, cases of varying sizes and an assortment of tools. Stretched securely across the rear exit doors were two large mattresses.

The men all were wearing the same standard sewermen's clothing: studded rubber thigh boots, seaman's socks, overalls, neck sweatband, safety belt and donkey jacket. In their hands or nearby each had a pair of protective gloves and a metal helmet.

Taylor checked his watch. "We should be in the West End now," he said.

Four minutes later Mike Daniels issued his first order. "Light the lamps."

Fagan was small and overweight but his hands were neat and his fingers surprisingly thin. His movements, as he opened the nine Spiralarm gas detector lamps and ignited the flame in each lamp, were short, sharp actions that combined and flowed together. His domed head was beginning to sweat and the loose flesh on his smooth face gave him the look of an intent baby old before its years.

In the cab of the van Cliff muttered, "Another twenty minutes should do it."

They took a direct route through Trafalgar Square, along The Strand and into Fleet Street. They crossed Ludgate Circus and went up the hill, past St. Paul's and into the City. The van made a left turn at the first set of major traffic lights. It went down the narrow side street, made a right turn, then another right which brought it traveling up a one-way street toward the main road again.

Cliff turned and slid back the partition behind his seat. He called through the space, "We're coming up to it." He closed the partition.

The five men in the van started to move into action. They put their gloves and helmets on and crouched tight in anticipation.

"Open it," Mike said.

Taylor moved to the round hole in the center of the floor and twisted the two bolt locks. He pulled out the cover and laid it to one side. Below him he could see the road. The van had reduced its speed to a crawl. Taylor waited. He saw the first chalk mark, then the second.

"Now," he said. One of the men banged on the partition and the van jerked to a halt. Taylor's head came away from the hole in the floor. "Half a foot more," he said.

The instruction was relayed through the partition and the van moved very slowly forward until it was exactly over the manhole cover in the road.

In the cab they waited for the final signal to be tapped on the partition. When it came, Cliff opened the passenger door and jumped out onto the road. The street was almost empty except for a few vans parked by the curb. The people who used the street as a shortcut to the main road took no notice of him as he slid his hand over the front offside tire. When he was sure of himself he gave the tire a hard slap with his hand and the spike, like a long, single knuckle-duster, pierced the rubber of the tire and the air hissed its escape.

The men inside heard the back doors of the van open and saw the streaks of light that came through the small gaps at the top and bottom of the mattresses. Cliff was taking out the spare wheel which had been fixed to one of the rear doors.

"Everything for real," Mike had said. "You never know but that some nut is looking out of an office window and wondering why the hell you're taking a perfectly good wheel off just to put it back on again."

Mike turned to them. "Now."

Taylor reached down through the hole to the manhole cover and with a sewerman's key engaged the cover. He reached his arm through the hole. The two men heaved and they heard the clank of the cover as they pulled it out of its housing and onto the road.

"The lamp."

Fagan took one of the Spiralarm lamps and lowered it through the hole and down into the manhole shaft. He let the cord through his hands slowly, watching for the white twist of rag that would tell him that the lamp was in the sewer.

"What happens if it comes up red?"

"Then we wait and try again," Mike told him.

Outside Gardner had put the hydraulic jack under the front of the van and was pumping it until the wheel was well off the floor.

Fagan lifted the lamp back up the shaft. "It's safe," he said as the lamp came into view, its small yellow flame flickering.

"Right," said Mike. "All in."

Fagan was the first one to squeeze through the hole. A large battery-powered lamp hung from his neck.

As Fagan's head disappeared into the shaft, Stephen stood waiting his turn. This was it, he thought. Once I'm into that shaft it's all the way. But there was no hesitation, he lowered himself down and then stood on the rungs of the ladder with only his head protruding into the van.

"The trolleys first," he said.

"That's right," said Taylor. "Down you go, one-nine."

Cliff stood by the van holding the spare wheel lazily against his leg. "I wouldn't go too fast," he said.

Stephen, Harry and Fagan stood in the blackness of the sewer. They were well rehearsed and there was no need for instructions. While Stephen waited, the other two hammered steel hooks into the brickwork from which they hung their lamps. The light from the lamps bounced off the rounded walls and cast dark, rippling shadows over the thick liquid that flowed gently up the sewer.

They unhooked the trolley and as the chain pulley went back up the shaft and into the van, they opened out the collapsible unit with its waterproof plastic sides and bottom. They found it was not difficult to push it through the shallow sewage. By the time they had erected the first, the other was on its way down the shaft.

Inside the van Mike Daniels and Taylor worked quickly. They were nearly finished. There was just one cylinder of oxyacetylene left. The only other things were the radio equipment, a collapsible chair, a table, two thermos flasks and some food containers. In the corner was a large, black leather tool bag: that was Mike's.

"I'll see you down there."

"Right," said Mike.

Taylor swung himself through the hole and disappeared into the shaft. He was halfway down the ladder when he started to shake. He stopped climbing and clutched at the steel rungs, pressing his body against them. His teeth were clenched, his eyes were closed and his breath was coming in short labored gasps. Slowly, with his body clinging to the ladder, he started to move.

He opened his eyes and kept them fixed rigidly on the rungs in front of him.

"You're nearly down," said Stephen.

"Got my bloody boot stuck," he said.

His body seemed light and uncoordinated. His hands felt the rough, brick sides of the sewer, which gave him confidence. He put his boot into the sewage as if testing out a hot bath.

"We're all ready to go," said Stephen.

The three trolleys stood loaded; on the front of the first hung two lamps and a Spiralarm lamp, its small flame burning yellow.

Gardner heard the signal as he was tightening the last of the wheel nuts. "That's it. They're done." He released the jack and the van dropped gently back onto the road. Cliff took the bench seat, put it inside the cab and then opened the partition, slipping into the back of the van.

"It's all yours," Mike said.

"Right."

Mike took the black bag with him and left it by the rim of the hole as he climbed through. Then he reached up to take it. "I'll be seeing you, kid."

"Yeah," said Cliff. "Have a good dig."

Cliff waited till Mike climbed down the ladder before he reached in and moved the manhole cover back into position.

The clanging of the cover echoed in the shaft and the blackness became more intense.

Up above Cliff checked the roadway; it was clear now.

Nothing was left to show that five men and a load of equipment had gone nearly twenty feet under London.

Cliff and Gardner moved up the street following the route the men underground would take and went past the bank.

"Lovely sight, isn't it?" said Cliff.

"Bend up ahead."

The three trolleys and the five men stopped. "We're right," said Daniels. "Keep going."

The line moved slowly because pushing the heavy trolleys through the water was not easy. It was difficult getting used to the cumbersome, studded boots, which occasionally slipped on the silt-covered bottom of the sewer.

"How much farther, Mike?"

"Not far, we're well under the main road now."

"Junction up ahead by the look of it."

"That'll be it."

"Thank Christ for that."

Their voices hung in the air, reverberating down the sewer, booming as the sound moved ahead of them.

Taylor was glad the sewer was not smaller. He couldn't have done it if it had been less than five feet. As it was, they all had to bend their heads to walk, even Harry and Fagan.

"Okay, we're here."

Mike left the trolley, took a lamp and walked ahead of the line to the junction.

"Bring that map up here, one-nine."

They opened it and held it between them. It showed the route from the entrance shaft to the junction and then beyond to a pumping station, or treatment works.

"The next shaft should only be a few yards farther on," Stephen said.

Mike moved back downstream to the men. "We'll set up here. Harry, the pontoon. Taylor, you and one-nine the lights and the alarm lamps."

The quiet sewer suddenly became alive as the men went to work. While the pontoon was pieced together and fixed securely into place across the width of the sewer, Mike unloaded the shoring units and digging tools and took them into the sewer through which they would have to tunnel.

Taylor and Stephen took the lamps and Spiralarms and fixed them onto the walls at intervals up and downstream from the pontoon.

"Just how good are those things?" said Harry.

"They're good," Taylor said. "Better than canaries. Just don't forget to watch 'em. If any of them lights go red, I want to know."

"I don't fancy gettin' meself gassed, mate."

"You finished, one-nine?"

"Yes."

"Let's measure up then and mark it out," said Mike.

As Stephen held the metal measuring tape where the two sewers joined, Mike moved up the second sewer, unreeling the tape as he went. When it was fully extended Stephen let it relax and followed it in. They repeated the process until they had measured out twelve feet six on the sewer wall.

In the light from the suspended lamp the compass showed NNE.

"Spot on. Fifteen foot in the chamber, then about two up. Sure you can get the angle right?"

Stephen grinned at him. "I'm sure," and he marked on the wall the spot where they would pull out the brickwork and start the tunnel.

"What time have we all got?" said Mike.

"I make it about two o'clock."

"Fourteen hundred hours, as we're operational," said Taylor.

"Well, I'd better be running out the phone line I suppose," Harry said.

"You need anyone to show you the way?"

"No thanks, I'll find it. Straight down past the bank, first right, then on for a hundred yards. Okay?"

"Take an alarm lamp."

Taylor watched Harry as he moved off down the sewer, glad that it was not him. The thought of being alone in the dark, damp, smelly underground tube made him shiver.

"Right. Let's go at it," said Mike.

"What's the time, Gardner?"

"Just after two."

The inside of the van looked like a radio controller's office. On the table was a VHF transmitter and receiver and next to it a sewerman's sound-powered telephone set. The lead from the telephone set coiled onto the floor and ran into a waterproof box that was covered in colored fluorescent plastic.

"Save a lot of aggravation if the radio worked underground."

"Well, it don't, so you're in for a cozy little time."

"Yeah. Might as well get it down."

Gardner had changed from his overalls into a dark blue suit, white shirt and dark tie. He looked like any of the men on the streets of the City of London.

He checked the radio equipment before he put it into his briefcase. Cliff opened the cover in the floor of the van, stretched down to the manhole cover directly beneath and with great effort moved the cover off, exposing the shaft that ran from the parking lot down into the sewers.

"Time to go," Gardner said. "How do I look?"

"Marvelous. Have a good day at the office, darlin'."

Gardner smiled at the boy and then very carefully opened the back door of the van. It was clear. He squeezed between the two mattresses and dropped lightly onto the ground. "I'll be talking to you."

Cliff closed and locked the doors behind him.

Gardner knew the old man at the entrance was still away having his lunch. He slipped out of the lot and onto the street. It was peculiar to walk free on the streets knowing that in the van and underground his mates were restricted. He could see the bank and the side street next to it, and he knew that twenty feet down they were working, far from the sun and noise. Farther down was the No Entry sign where earlier he had changed the wheel.

The office building was old. The first three floors were taken up by an insurance company, the other two floors were small office suites. He took the ancient elevator to the fifth floor. The two good-looking birds who got in with him smiled as they stepped out at the third floor. He thought it was a pity he wouldn't be seeing them again.

For a furnished office it was pretty crummy: two beat-up 1930's desks with a couple of wooden swivel chairs and a tattered sofa, a line of ex–war office filing cabinets and net curtains that would fall apart if anyone ever thought to wash them.

But it wasn't very important, not for their purposes. He went over to the window and looked out across the street: a beautiful sight—a clear uninterrupted view. He could see the main door and the entrance in the side street. It was perfect.

"Dirty bastards." Harry saw the flash of ugly, yellow eyes and heard the squeak and splash as a pair of rats scampered away, frightened by the beam of light. He waited until he was sure they had gone before he moved on. The new sewer was much smaller than the main one they were working in, about four feet six high and not much wider than three feet.

His lamp caught the telephone line in its beam. It was hanging by a rope suspended about a foot above the water, shining bright orange.

Above, in the van, Cliff sat by the circular hole in the floor like an Eskimo ice fishing. He looked down into the blackness of the shaft and could see Harry's light moving about. The lamp light shone straight up into his face and he waved. Then it was gone and the rope hung slack. He pulled it and the line from the telephone that Harry would be letting out from the box as he walked back down the sewer. He heaved the manhole cover back into position and placed a wedge under it so that its weight would not cut into the wire.

Harry was glad to turn the corner into the larger sewer. It was tricky holding the lamp in one hand and the Spiralarm round his neck, seeing that the line ran smoothly from the box and not falling into the shit all at the same time.

Harry thought to himself, Bloody glad I don't have to do that one over again. Don't know how them blokes stand it working down here all the bleedin' time. Wonder how much they make, twenty, thirty nicker a week? He laughed to himself. Not as much as we're going to have and that's a certainty. He had not thought out what he was going to do with his share.

Maybe Taylor would have him on one of them planes: quick flip across the water into Belgium. Very nice that would be. On the other hand he might do better on his own.

Gardner moved the desk and the sofa against the window and, considering the circumstances, it was not too uncomfortable to sit and look down at the bank. On the desk top he had laid out the VHF equipment and his food and drink.

Very carefully he wiped the lenses of the Zeiss 1050 binoculars and adjusted the focus. The people on the other side of the road going into the bank jumped ten times in size.

Better give young Cliff a call and test the old waves out, he said to himself. "Rover to base, Rover to base, over."

"Base to Rover. Loud and clear, over."

"How's the passenger situation, base, over."

"Your next passenger not called yet," Cliff said. Stand by, out."

What were they doing down there? Gardner wondered. He poured himself a cup of black coffee from the thermos flask and rummaged in the bottom of the brief-case for the copies of *Playboy*. Then he lay on the sofa, looked through the magazines and waited.

Harry could see the lights from the pontoon reflecting in the water. He pushed through the water more quickly now, letting out the line as he went.

"What's going on here?" he said.

Taylor was sitting on the pontoon drinking a mug of tea. There was no sign of the others.

"Tea break. I'm waiting for the first trolley."

Harry hung up his lamps, put the orange box on the pontoon and started to unwrap it, tearing open the thick cardboard. He let the covering and the box float away on the sewage. He put the gray telephone unit onto the pontoon.

"Don't know if I'll be able to eat anything down here."

"Why not?"

"It's the atmosphere."

"Try a cuppa tea," Taylor said.

"Well, all right. I could bloody use something."

They could hear the sounds coming from the other sewer.

"Sounds like someone's digging," Harry said.

"Yeah, they made a good start."

"Thought you was goin' to be in there."

"I decided to change over," said Taylor. "Reckoned it would be better if I was around here at the nerve center. Keep an eye on things. Here's your tea."

A circle of bricks had been torn away from the side of the sewer where Stephen had marked the wall. He stood resting and watching as Mike swung the pick into the mud. Fagan was clearing back the debris from the digging and shoveling it into one of the trolleys.

Mike let the pick drop to the ground. Then he lifted his neckband and wiped the sweat from his face.

"Let's have a breather. I want to see if Harry's back with that phone."

"It's my turn anyway," Stephen said and he took the pick from Mike.

"Gets bloody hot down here." He left and pushed through the water back to the pontoon.

"Got that telephone working yet?"

"Hello, Mike. Just gonna do the test."

"I'll have some of that tea," he said to Taylor.

Harry twisted the circular mouthpiece of the telephone unit and waited. In the van Cliff heard the buzz and lifted the receiver.

"Hello."

"Pontoon to Cliff, how're you doing?"

"All right, mate. What's it like down there?"

"Bloody lovely. You don't know what you're missing."

Mike gulped down his tea. "Tell him it's almost closing time."

"Kid, Mike says it's time the old jug was closing. Better give Rover a call."

"Roger, pontoon, over and out." The line went dead. Cliff turned to the transmitter. "Base to Rover, over." He waited. "Base to Rover, over." There was still no reply. Where the fuck is he? he thought. "Base to Rover, base to Rover, where are you, over?"

Gardner's voice came over breathless as he answered.

"Rover to base, over."

"Where the hell have you been, Rover?"

"I had to pee."

"That's the trouble with you old men. Can't hold your water. Your passenger called up. Wants to know if it's free."

"Hold on, base."

Gardner turned to the window and without using the binoculars he could see that the bank had closed its doors. He went back to the transmitter.

"You there, base?"

"Go ahead, Rover."

"Last drinks all round."

"Roger, over and out."

Harry put the receiver down.

"Well, they're shut all right," he said.

"Okay." Mike turned to Taylor. "There'll be a full trolley up there now."

"Right," Taylor said. "We put the stuff up the shaft?"

"Yeah. There'll be some bricks in the first lot so you can build it up nicely. Just take it as high as you can. Then we'll dump the rest of it on the bottom and let the water carry it away."

Taylor slipped off the pontoon into the water and waded up the other sewer. He thought he was getting used to it at last and that it might not be so bad for him. As long as he didn't feel crowded, he'd be all right.

"No trouble, was there?"

"Saw a couple of rats. That's about all," Harry said.

"Well, have a rest. You'd better check the lamps."

"I was going to ask Mike what happens if we bump into any real sewermen?"

"You won't meet any sewermen whatsoever, Harry, believe me. An' by happy coincidence they knock off just after the jug closes. Very tidy."

"I'll be off then," Harry said.

Mike passed Taylor, who waited with the trolley until he had gone by. They did not say anything to each other and Taylor went on down the sewer toward the pontoon.

"How's it going?" Mike said.

"I think we're just about ready to fit the first bit of shoring," Stephen said.

"It looks as if it could hold up well without it, doesn't it?"

"Well, maybe it would," said Stephen. "But I think we'd feel a little more confident with it than without, don't you?"

"Me, I bloody would, I'll tell you that for nothing," said Fagan.

"Let's get at it then."

They had dug about four feet into the thick City mud and the hole was just over three feet square. Stephen took one of the prefabricated aluminum shoring units and three of the foot-wide aluminum planks from the container that was leaning against the wall of the sewer. The sewer water made an eddy around the container.

"Get the jack, will you."

He went to the entrance of the tunnel and opened out the unit—it was a good fit. He took the jack from Fagan and started pumping up the center V as it straightened out, so the uprights of the unit bit into the mud walls of the tunnel.

"Hammer."

The center piece was horizontal and he began to hit it with the hammer, first the left side, then the right until the whole arm had moved up to the ceiling.

"Added a little refinement," he said. "Pass me that cross-piece, Fagan."

The bar of aluminum rod fit exactly between the uprights and he knocked it between them and into the floor of the tunnel.

"Now the roofing."

Fagan slid three one-foot pieces of metal into the gap between the top cross-member and the mud roof so that they lay side by side, forming a solid metal ceiling to the tunnel. Then Stephen banged the horizontal bar home. He crawled back into the sewer.

"There you are. Safe as houses, literally. As we go farther in the ceiling strips'll overlap, so there won't be any doubt they'll hold."

"It's bloody marvelous, one-nine," Mike said. "I tell you I don't think I would have had the patience. Bloody marvelous."

"Well, we didn't want the roof to fall in, did we?"

"How far to go?" said Fagan.

"About eleven feet. Digging out a decent-sized chamber'll take some time. And remember the deeper we go, the more difficult it'll be to move out the loose mud."

"We're not pushed for time anyway," said Mike. "We've got tonight and all weekend if necessary."

"In that case," said Fagan, "how about a little sustenance?"

The five men gathered around the pontoon, glad to rest.

"Harry, you be mother and pour the tea."

"Oh, charmin'."

"There more mugfuls, then it's on to the soft drinks. Who wants a bit of grub?" said Harry. He opened the plastic food containers and handed them out without waiting for the replies.

"Very good menu here: cold chicken, baked beans and a little sausage. And no complaints or you can pop out an' get your own."

"Who's kosher?" said Fagan. "And where's the telly?"

"You know what we're missing tonight, don't you?" Stephen said.

"What?"

" 'Mission Impossible.' "

They began to laugh and it was infectious—the relief from tension. Only Mike seemed to be apart from them, managing a smile, but nothing more.

"Okay, hold it down for Christ's sake," he said.

The sound of their noise and laughter reverberated through the sewer and he was suddenly worried that it would carry outside the sewer.

In the van Cliff dozed, his head down in his arms, his hair spilling onto the table, the transmitter and telephone close so that if they were activated he would hear them.

On the fifth floor behind the locked doors of the rented office suite, Gardner opened a bottle of Coke. He had pushed up the old-fashioned windows and the stuffy air and cigarette smoke floated into the warm afternoon.

It seemed as if there was a common timetable being kept: at certain times they all took a break. It was the natural rhythm of action and inaction. In the sewer there was continual work to be done, but for the two men aboveground the time of real contribution would be concentrated into a short, very active and vital schedule. They would report to the ones below of the hectic comings and goings, the timing of the enemy, or anything unexpected.

Stephen thought it was like a workmen's outing: you expected them to break open a barrel of beer and start the dirty stories. It was fantastic when you considered it—there they were preparing to blow themselves into a vault that held a fortune and you would think from the way they were acting that it was nothing more important than a day down the mines. He felt that way himself and it was more than he could comprehend. Stealing thousands he could understand: he knew what you could do with that kind of money. But a hundred thousand or more, what about that? What did it look like? How much space would it take up? Where would he keep it? You couldn't really wander into a bank and say, "Oh, yes, good morning, I'd want to open an account and here's a suitcase full just to start things off."

He remembered Jennifer and wondered how on earth he was going to explain it to her. He began to imagine driving home with a car full of cash.

Leave the car in the garage at night, and when she and the children were asleep, creep out to get it? Then what? Hide it under the floorboards in the attic? It would give him perpetual nightmares of the house burning down.

How would he explain the change in their standard of living? How to conceal it? Spend it? Perhaps the worst thing of all, not being able to tell. When a man accomplishes something, he wants the whole world to know, and the more people who praise him the better. But not this. It would have to be a secret forever.

"Harry, clear up here, will you."

"It'll be a pleasure. Do you want me to check them lamps again, Mike?"

"Every half-hour. You don't have to ask."

The break was over and it was back to reality.

"Get on the phone, Fagan, and get me a weather forecast."

"The weather? What's with the weather?"

"Just find out and let me know."

They went back to dig and drag out the loose mud and load it on the trolley so that the entrance to the shaft nearest them could be blocked, just in case anyone slipped. It was a hard, hot, tiring job and they took it in shifts. Mike and Stephen, then Fagan and Taylor, who made excuses and did not do any of the digging. A change had come over him; he had lost his sense of command and they noticed and resented it.

"Who wants to be a millionaire?" Harry sang. "I do. Who wants da da dada de. I do." He was feeling very much all right. His off-key voice echoed up the sewer and he swung his lamp so that the reflections on the water jumped and bounced off the walls.

He thought he was having it quite easy, really, every half hour up and downstream to check the alarm lamps and in between giving a hand to shift the mud—a breeze when he considered that Mike and Stephen spent most of their time in the tunnel. They were over nine feet in and shoring up as if it were a gold mine.

He was getting tired. It's this rotten bleedin' air down here, he thought. Be glad to get back up top. His legs dragged in the sewage and he shook his head because his eyes had suddenly become heavy and the lids kept dropping.

He was almost on top of the lamp before he saw it and then it took him a peculiar, disoriented time to focus and realize that it was burning red.

"Oh fuck, fucking 'ell." He turned, slipped on the silt and crashed into the sewage. The lamp went under the surface and the light from its watertight shell sent bent, wavy shafts through the water. He dragged himself up and lunged forward, slipped again and bounced from wall to wall in the frenzy and panic of trying to run from something he couldn't see.

His voice was a low gurgled croak as he tried to shout, "Mike, Mike for fuck's sake."

Taylor was pushing the trolley back from the shaft when he saw the crazy swinging of the light coming at him from beyond the pontoon. Then he saw the shit and grime-covered figure and the mouth that was trying to spit out the vomit and words.

"Jesus Christ, Mike, Fagan." His voice screeched the words, "Mike, Mike."

Mike came from the upper sewer. The water splashed in front of him as he tried to run. He saw Taylor's white, drawn face, Harry's smeared stinking features and the red lamp almost all at the same time.

"Get the masks." Taylor moved with him and they tore at the container of tubes and bottles and masks for the oxygen equipment.

As Harry collapsed in the sewage the rats overcame their fright. There were at least six of them—a family. They hit him as his limp body dragged against the bottom of the sewer, going for his face.

Stephen and Fagan felt the tightness grab at their lungs as they fought with their slowing muscles to get the masks on.

The rats squeaked and tried to scamper into the darkness but the gas was affecting them too. The men beat at them with picks and chisels and there was a frenzy of splashing red water as they hit and hit and hit.

Taylor and Mike pulled Harry's limp body from the sewage, dragged it up onto the pontoon and got an oxygen mask on him. Then all they could do was wait.

Suddenly it was calm. There was nothing to be done. They stood watching the red lamps that told them there was a drifting, invisible killer in the sewer.

Daniels took his gloves off and felt for Harry's pulse. At first he thought it had gone, but then as he moved his fingers over the wrist, he found it: a slow dim beat.

He felt someone knock his arm and point up the sewer. The lamp farthest away from them had turned from red back to yellow. Then the next lamp changed and the next, then the one opposite them. It was as if a ghost were passing down the sewer.

Mike Daniels lifted the mask from his face and while the others waited he sniffed at the stale air. The gas had gone, passing on its lethal way to other tunnels.

All the masks were off and they could only stand in numbed silence. The danger had passed but it had changed the men.

They turned to Harry.

It was Taylor who tore the mask off his face and loosened the neckband. The face was gray and through the slime and stink were the blood-red bite marks the rats had made.

Fagan turned away. His stomach heaved and bile

came into his mouth. He leaned against the sewer wall and vomited into the sewage.

"Get the brandy and the first-aid kit." Taylor's voice was cold, unemotional and confident. Out of the disaster had come a renewal of his ability to lead. It had affected him physically. His athlete's body was tall and straight again and his actions smooth and controlled.

He doused the cotton wool with the brandy and washed the excrement from Harry's face, away from his mouth and out of his eyes. He cleaned the bites and then, when the skin was clean again, he put his mouth over Harry's and began to give the kiss of life.

The men could do nothing—they could not go back to the work without knowing. So they stood there watching Taylor.

"He's coming out of it." Taylor stood back and they could see that the face was losing the dead grayness and that under the overalls the lungs were pumping on their own. Taylor gently lifted Harry's head and poured some of the brandy through the almost bloodless lips. It made him cough and splutter, but there, twenty feet down in the sewer, it was like seeing a newborn child smacked by the doctor and hearing the cry that means life.

Taylor covered the rat bites with antiseptic gauze, then strips of waterproof adhesive. He put a towel from the first-aid box under Harry's head and moved the boxes that had not been knocked into the sewer around the limp figure. "That's all we can do." He turned to Mike.

"He should go back up and get to a doctor."

They all knew there was no answer to that.

"Within twelve hours maybe," Mike said. "Sooner with luck."

The buzz from the sound-powered telephone shook the atmosphere. Mike looked at the receiver and let it buzz again before he lifted it.

"What is it, kid?"

"The weather bureau says it's continuing warm with maybe some thunder showers. An' Gardner says they've knocked off for the day except, by his count, three of 'em including the manager. Probably clocking up a piece of overtime."

"Aren't we all," Mike said.

The conversation finished, Mike turned to them. "Time's creeping on. Most of them have gone home." He stretched his body and took in deep breaths of the new uncontaminated air.

"Right, okay, we're one short now. Taylor, you clear up here an' take over watching them lamps. You'd better have the breathing gear with you."

Gardner relayed every visible move that was made. How many in, how many out. The manager and the other two left for the weekend. Get a shock on Monday morning they would, Gardner thought. The manager'll get his a bit sooner.

Since there was no word from down under everything must be all right or he'd have heard. He wondered how far in they were. By late evening it should all be ready, then the fireworks would start.

He marked down the time the first security van arrived but there would be no routine. They might come back in half an hour or longer—you couldn't tell.

Mike Daniels was a very clever man, he thought. In fifteen years of thieving he'd only done one bit of bird which was slightly better than most. Mike was dead cool and he knew what he was doing. Very good reputation he had.

The warm, slightly heavy summer evening drifted by. The City had emptied and took on a quietness, now that the day's business was over. There were no strip clubs or skin-flick cinemas, and only a few restaurants. It was a peaceful place to walk in the evenings or the weekend. There was St. Paul's to see and the river and the monument and the Bank of England. Then, to find some life, back to Ludgate Circus and up Fleet Street.

The first security check was over and the janitors had finished up and gone.

The action would not start for a few hours but anything that happened now was important, so he kept close watch.

They were exhausted.

Taylor and Fagan had cleared a place for themselves on the pontoon so that they could stretch out. Harry had hardly moved, still stunned from the shock of the gas and the rats.

The tunnel was complete and they had dug out a chamber. Unlike the tunnel there had to be room to maneuver.

Their clothes were wet and stained with the mud and shit of the sewer and their faces were streaked with dirt and sweat. The physical effort and the tension had drained them.

In the chamber Mike and Stephen sat on the wooden planks they used to line the floor and leaned back against the thick, solid mud walls of the chamber. The light from the lamp cast sharp, black shadows and heightened the drawn furrows under their eyes and cheekbones.

It was still. The only sound was of the sewage as it moved around the legs of the pontoon and the cylinders. When one of the men at the pontoon coughed, it made a dull echo that was carried up the tunnel and into the chamber.

"We could all use some sleep." Stephen's voice was hoarse.

"A rest'll have to do."

Stephen stretched and sighed. "I think I'll go back down and have the last of that tea and something to eat."

The two men crawled into the tunnel and like soldiers on an obstacle course wriggled over the wet, slippery mud floor down the slight gradient to the sewer. They could see the light hanging on the wall at the mouth of the tunnel.

"How's he doing?" Mike said.

"Still in a sort of coma," Taylor said.

"Any tea?"

"Yeah, there's a drop left, I think."

"All done?" Fagan asked.

"Yeah, just got to clear the mud off the ceiling and there it is, hardcore and the reinforced concrete. Any word from up top?"

"The security mob have been back a couple of times. Now it's all clear."

Stephen had poured the mugs of tea, passing one to Mike and then the last of the food from the containers.

"We got plenty of line for that phone? It's got to reach right the way up into the vault."

"Yeah," Taylor said. "I mean I measured it out, a good thirty feet."

Mike looked over the rim of the mug at him. He had to have it out in the open. "How you going to be, up there?" He inclined his head to the tunnel.

Taylor had wondered when something was going to be said. Christ, he thought, what do you fucking do when you find out you've got something in you you don't know how to control?

"Never had it before, you know. Just came over, just like that."

"It's claustrophobia," Stephen said.

"I know what it fucking is."

"What about the tunnel?"

He looked at Mike again. "I don't know," he paused. "I don't reckon it's on."

"No nor do I. You'll miss a lovely sight."

"Well, I'll have to do without it, won't I?"

"What about him going up and swapping with the youngster?" Fagan had the look of a man who had surprised himself with his own brilliance.

"No," Mike said. "That's not how we figured it. It wouldn't work. We'll have to be one short in the vault, that's all. There'll be enough to do out here."

"It's not my bleeding fault, I didn't fucking do it on purpose for Christ's sake," Taylor said. His voice had a defensive, angry whine.

"I know you didn't," Mike said quickly. "Just a bit hard, that's all."

He put the mug down. "Clear up here and get the stuff ready. Fagan, I want an alarm lamp this side of the tunnel and one in the chamber."

They moved and the rest time was over. The weakness in Taylor had given them strength, as if one weak link was all they knew they could afford.

"Clean the last of the mud off that ceiling, one-nine. Then have a go at crashing some of that hardcore away."

147

There was action again: the stillness was broken. Taylor accepted his relegation and after clearing away the mugs, checked over the drilling equipment. He left it ready to be taken up the tunnel.

There was a street lamp right outside the bank. Very useful that is, Gardner said to himself. He had to use the binoculars all the time now, but the view was perfect. The empty street helped. When the security men came it was easy for him to count them in and out. They had been the same men every time so far and he wondered when they changed shifts.

Way over the rooftops a light came on in a room at the top of a building. He readjusted the focus and brought the image up sharp. It was a woman standing by the curtained windows, and he could just see the furniture of a bedroom.

She opened one of the windows, leaned out and looked over the City. She was a blonde and the movement of her body was slow and casual.

The woman stepped back from the window into the bedroom light and started to unzip her dress. She let it drop to the floor and disappeared from view as she bent down to pick it up.

She stood in front of the long mirror of a wardrobe and studied her figure. She was just a bit heavy, big bosoms, a bit thick round the middle. Then she reached behind her back and unhooked the white bra. "Move over darling," Gardner said. "Go on. That's it."

She turned to look at her profile and he could see her big breasts that sagged just a little. She cupped her hands under them, lifting them slightly, playing with them, moving them around. Her hands were on her hips and it looked like she was going to take her knickers off. "Go on darlin', that's lovely." Her hands moved under the waistband and then slid down over her thighs, taking the pants with them. She had to bend over and Gardner could see her ass. He was pressed up against the window-sill and he felt himself very hard.

"Bleedin' exercises," he said. "I got an exercise I could show you." She was swinging her arms, bending again, to a rhythm. Her legs were wide apart and as she swung her arms around, her hips moved and her breasts were bouncing. At that distance she was without a blemish.

His eyes started to glaze and the image blurred.

"Jeesus." He looked down into the street. The security van was parked outside the bank. He brought the binoculars round and saw the driver standing on the street, smoking. The door of the bank was open.

He turned to the VHF set and, as if they had just arrived, passed the information. Then he went back to the window and waited.

They were coming out now, locking the door, climbing back into the van. He glanced across toward the window. All he could see were the black outlines of the buildings. "She must have gone to bed. Just as well."

He was sweating. That's my one mistake, he said to himself. Just one—that's all you get.

The floor of the chamber was covered by the rubble of hardcore Stephen had hacked away from underside the reinforced concrete base of the vault. He used the shovel to push it down the tunnel and rake it into the sewage.

"Tell Mike it's all ready," he said. He sat and rested in the chamber. This is where it could go terribly wrong, he thought. Then what, escape? A rush through the sewage to the shaft? Or on farther to another shaft? Mike had said there were more exits than the combined members of the Metropolitan and City police forces. It sounded good but he knew theory was one thing and practice another.

He heard Mike crawling up the tunnel. "All set, one-nine?" he said. He had changed into a leather suit and in his hand he carried a visor that would completely cover his head.

"Yes," he answered, "it's all yours."

"Yeah, well, seems okay, enough room. Just hope your calculations are right."

"Don't worry about that. It's the rest of it that makes me a bit shaky."

Mike slapped him on the leg. "Ah, don't you get nervous, one-nine. This is my specialty, remember? I'll tell you something," he said. "This is the part I like best."

"I'm glad you feel happy about it."

Stephen went down the tunnel to the pontoon.

"He's ready for the stuff, Fagan."

"Right. I'll need a hand, Taylor. Up to the tunnel anyway."

The two men started to manhandle the equipment: a generator that would supply power to an extractor fan, a thermic lance holder and the ten-foot rods it would burn, the oxyacetylene cutter and then the cylinders of oxygen and acetylene. When Stephen had changed into his leather suit he pulled up the telephone and the coils of lead.

Taylor was standing at the mouth of the tunnel. He set up the generator and the connections to the cylinders. The coils of tubing disappeared into the tunnel.

"Fagan's up there," he said. "You'll have to wait. No room for three of you and that stuff, I shouldn't think."

Fagan came into the sewer, feet first, crawling backward. "Up the tunnel of love, one-nine," he said.

"See you later."

"Yeah. Don't bleedin' blow yourself up, will you?"

Stephen turned. "I'll do my best not to."

Mike was waiting for him.

"It's all marked out," he said.

Stephen looked at the ceiling. A circle of punch holes had been made, about twenty of them, and in the center another, larger punch mark.

"I've done the rods, nicely bent, at the correct angle," Mike said. He was enjoying himself.

"How do you know when you're at the right depth?"

"Experience, that's all. Six inches in all round and eight for the center hole. Just hope that concrete don't crack before we're ready. One peep of air into that vault and off we go. Rather not have the alarm belling away until I'm ready."

"We wouldn't hear it anyway, would we?" Stephen said.

"No, we wouldn't. But we'd soon find out. Get Fagan a few feet in and let him have that phone. I want an open line to Cliff. You know where you've gotta be, right behind ready with those rods. They don't take long to burn down."

Cliff nearly jumped when the buzzer went. "Hello, what's up?" He snapped out of his hazy half-sleep. He and Gardner were part of it at last. They were important; controllers in a way, and if they said stop, then stop it would be and no mucking about.

"Right," he said and attached the headset to the telephone. Then he called Rover Gardner on the radio.

"Rover to base, receiving you, over."

"What's the traffic situation, Rover, over?"

"Very clear, over."

"Keep the line open, Rover, and stand by, out."

"It's all clear," Fagan said.

"Check the lamps again."

"No problem."

The tiredness and apathy had gone. They were alert, ready. This was what all the hours of preparation and work had been about.

Mike smiled and picked up his visor. "I'd put yours on if I were you. Before you light that burner."

Stephen held the oxyacetylene torch in his hand and checked the Spiralarm lamp that hung from a hook they had driven into the mud. The flame was still yellow and he hoped to God it was accurate. He pulled the visor over his head and snapped the lighter. His hands were clumsy in the rubber gloves and it took him a couple of tries before the flame ignited.

He rested the lighter on the floor boards, put the nozzle of the torch to it and turned the control knobs. It caught and he adjusted the mixture until the flame was white and hard. The relief he felt was fantastic; there had been no explosion. Then he passed the torch to Mike who held the flame to the end of the thermic lance rod, waiting for the heat to rise to 900 degrees centigrade, the point at which the rod tip would glow. Then he would let the oxygen in and watch the temperature zoom to around 3,500 degrees as the steel was eaten away.

It would drive those vault makers round the bend. There they have a nice uncrackable vault and up come the boffins with the old lance, coming up through the floor—lovely.

Mike had conned his way into a demonstration once that made his mouth water: a group stood outside a vault and a fellow got going with the lance. It took him seconds to burn through the layers of steel—like cutting butter, it was. But of course being a security demo the alarm had gone right off, and it would now, too.

It took about ninety seconds to burn out the first six-inch-deep hole, by which time the chamber and tunnel looked like a dust storm had hit it. The intense heat caused the breakdown of the concrete and turned it into lava which flowed down the mud walls to the floor.

Fagan had passed the fan up the tunnel to Stephen and it helped to circulate the thick, black fog. But it was in their eyes and nostrils and throats. As each rod burned away, Stephen fed another to Mike. Everything was by feel, touch, for it was useless trying to see through the smoke.

Five rods to go, Mike thought, Christ I'll be glad when this lot's over and done. He was on the last three when he felt Stephen pulling on his leg. It was the danger signal; the bleeding security mob must have arrived again. It wasn't the alarm, it couldn't be. He kept going, two more. With the open line they would have been told the second the van pulled up outside the bank. They probably wouldn't be able to hear Cliff anyway; the noise from the generator was like a speed boat turning over.

One more—he'd have to risk it. Eight inches this time, he nearly forgot. He cut the oxygen. Taylor must have turned off the generator since he couldn't hear it. He started to crawl backward down the tunnel leaving the lance and everything behind. He prayed that floor base held. He felt his legs come to the drop at the mouth of the tunnel where it fell to the sewage level. That's it, he could feel his legs in the water; he was out.

He stood up, took off the visor and blinked. It still

was like a London smog but it was clearing. The draft in the sewer was lifting the atmosphere and taking it downstream. It was so thick you could see the air move.

Taylor passed him the bottle of brandy, but the way his throat felt, he would have drunk the bloody sewer water if there'd been nothing else.

"I never seen nothing like it," Taylor said. "It's a bleeding wonder you didn't flake out, the lot of you. Bloody hell."

"What's up?" Harry shouted. "Where are they, where are they? The bastards, the bloody fucking bastards." The pitch of his voice was higher with every word.

"Jesus, hold him down. It's all right, Harry, it's all right. Lie back, boy, that's it, it's all right."

"Give 'im some of that brandy, for Christ's sake."

"Here, Harry, have some of this. There, that's better, isn't it?"

"Oh, bloody hell, I didn't know where I was. What's up then? Eh, what's up?"

His voice was rising again and Mike went over to the pontoon and looked down at him. "It's all right, Harry, you don't have to worry. Been out for a spell you have, but it's all right now."

"Hello, Mike," he said. "You all right then, are you? That's good. Christ, I don't half feel fucking awful."

"Just rest, Harry. You stay right here. We won't be too long now and you can have a breather. Just rest, that's all."

Harry sank back on the pontoon. The exertion had

exhausted him and his breathing became regular as he drifted off again into a deep sleep.

"Poor bastard," said Taylor.

"Where's that phone?"

"I'm sorry," said Stephen. "I left it up the tunnel. I'll get it."

The tunnel was still choked with concrete dust. Stephen had the phone line in his hand and as he crawled forward he held onto it, following it to the source.

He heard Cliff's faint yelling coming from the receiver before his hand reached it. He coughed as he spoke. "Hello, Cliff."

"What the bloody hell's been going on? I been trying to raise you for bleeding hours."

"Everything's fine." He coughed again.

"You got a bleeding cold, one-nine?"

"No," Stephen said. "It's the dust. How's everything up there?"

"It's all right. They've pissed off now. It's all clear."

"Great. Okay, Cliff. We'll close down for a time. I'll buzz you back."

Stephen found both parts of the phone and dragged them out of the tunnel with him.

"They've gone."

"Thank Christ for that," Mike said. "I gotta get this leather off. It's like a desert inside here."

He peeled off the leather suit and opened the jacket of the sewerman's overalls and flapped it in the still air.

"That's better," he said. "I'd get yours off if I was you, one-nine."

"Shall I start that fan up again, Mike?" Fagan asked.

"Maybe you should. It's bad enough down here without having the air full of shit as well. Talk about bleeding pollution. They should have a basinful of this muck."

Fagan went into the other sewer and they heard the pop, pop of the generator pack as he started it up. For a time the air got thicker as the fan drew the dust out of the tunnel.

"Let's have a walk upstream, one-nine. We can get some slightly fresh air and check the lamps at the same time."

Mike turned to Taylor. "Do 'em downstream, will you, mate?"

They parted and Taylor went off on his own. He walked slowly through the sewage, swinging the lamp ahead to scare the rats.

"That's the worst of it, over," Mike said.

"Hold this, will you?" Stephen passed him the light and then bent over to pull up the tops of his rubber thigh boots.

"What about the blasting?" he said.

"Nothing to it. One small charge in the middle'll bring the whole bloody slab down. Then it's all in for the lucky dip."

They were like two men out for a stroll down a country lane at night. Mike holding the light, Stephen behind him, hands in pockets.

Both alarm lamps, hanging on their hooks in the wall, glowed yellow. The sewer was free of gas.

"Let's go on a bit," Mike said. "I could use the exercise."

They walked the length of the sewer up to the shaft. Mike stepped out of the sewage onto the flat chamber. He switched the lamp off and then put it down on the floor of the chamber. Thin streams of light came down the shaft through the grill in the road above them.

"Daylight already. Don't worry," he said, "I'm only going up to get a taste of fresh air."

Stephen watched him climb the metal ladder, step over step until he was touching the underside of the grill. Mike held onto the ladder and looked down at the small, dark figure below. He breathed in the draft of clean air. "It's like a tonic, Stephen," he said. "Pity we can't take some of it back to Harry."

He stayed there for about five minutes before he came down to the chamber. He told Stephen that he should have a turn. It would do him good.

Stephen touched the grill, careful not to push his fingers through it so that they would show on the road-way. Mike was right. The London air they said was so polluted tasted clean and pure. One big heave, he thought, and he could be back on the street, free, away from it all.

He looked at his watch, amazed that it was nearly six o'clock. No wonder it was so quiet. There wouldn't be much traffic in the City that early on a Saturday morning.

God, he thought, I was getting out of bed this time yesterday. Jennifer had been close to him, warm, soft and smiling. He had tried not to wake her but she had turned in the bed, half-awake. Her arms went around his neck and she pulled him back and kissed him.

He had cooked himself an egg and some bacon and made strong black coffee. The memory was so sharp he could almost smell that breakfast up there at the grill.

There had been no need for him to get up that early but he'd always made sure he had time to spare for appointments. He had sipped the hot coffee and smoked the day's first cigarette and thought it was a damn funny life. Three months ago his self-pity had nearly pushed him over the edge. Now he was getting ready to steal a few million pounds.

Mike spat into the dark water. It's not going to be easy with Harry like he is, he thought. They'd leave all the gear, give old Bill a lesson or two and make a nice story for the papers. But they had to carry the cash and it would take two of them to get Harry through the sewer. Then they'd have the ladder to worry about.

Very inconvenient it was going to be. Still, they couldn't leave the poor bastard. On top of that there was Taylor. He'd reckoned there would be four in the vault with a fifth in the chamber helping pack and staying by that phone. Now because that fine athletic specimen had come down with a nice case of claustrophobia they were down to three.

They should have all the time in the world; the vault was not going to open its doors until the time lock went on Monday morning. Only he should get Harry out soon. Bit of a problem that was.

He watched Stephen climbing slowly down the ladder. Funny how a straight guy like him should turn out to be so good. Bet he was a marvelous architect. They shouldn't have let him go. He'd never really cared too much about the others he'd worked with but he was a bit fond of Stephen. Hope he comes out of it all right, he thought. Wouldn't like to see him in the nick—kill him, it would.

"Feeling better, then?" Mike asked.

"Yes, I am. You going to let the other two off for a bit? They need it as much as we did."

"If they want. Taylor might not fancy it too much though, might he?"

"Shall we get back?"

"Might as well," Mike said and he switched the lamp on again.

As they came into the circles of light around the pontoon they could see that the fan had done a good job and the air was nearly back to normal.

"Taylor," Mike said. "Why don't you try a turn up the road with Fagan. Do you a load of good if you was to go up the ladder for some air."

"I'll stay with you if you like," said Fagan.

"All right then," Taylor said. "I don't mind giving it a go."

Fagan picked up a lamp. "I'll lead on, shall I?"

"Tea all gone, has it?" Mike asked.

Stephen shook the thermos flasks. "Yes."

"Well, how about a Coke then? There's a crate over back there."

They sat on the pontoon drinking Coke from bottles. Occasionally Harry would murmur and move in his sleep. "He doesn't seem to be coming round in a hurry, does he?" Mike said.

"What will you do with him?"

"Well, once we're out of here Gardner can take care of him. They're quite close, those two. Been working together for years. Long before I met them."

"What are you planning to do after?" Stephen asked him.

"Going off with my family. Clearing out. It's the only way. With you it's different. You got no record. That makes it very difficult for old Bill, unless you got captured or started flashing the readies all over the place. But they know me, so when they tumble onto this one they're not going to be very happy and they'll be turning over a few places. It's all a question of elimination. There's only about six blokes who could rig this job. Half of them'll be in the nick so that leaves three. They'll be knocking on my door straight away. Only I won't be there."

"It seems awful, having to run," Stephen said.

"I got it all organized anyway. With a bit of luck Sunday night could see me halfway across Europe."

"I've thought about that myself," Stephen said.

"There's no need. You know what I was thinking?

Bloody funny it would be. You should take all your cash, split it up into nice round sums and open a few safety deposit accounts. You know, put it back where you got it from. If it were me I couldn't resist opening one here. I'd really like that."

Stephen laughed. You couldn't help admiring him, he thought. Not with a sense of humor like that, so bloody cheeky.

"Only thing is," Mike said, "you can't take out any insurance on that sort of money. Like the stuff we're going to get: I bet half of it is fiddled. Nobody puts cash in a deed box, not unless they don't want anyone to know about it. I tell you, up above it's all going on only they don't call it stealing. Should make you feel better. I mean it's only taking what someone else thieved in the first place."

"You're making me feel like Robin Hood already," said Stephen.

They heard the other two wading back through the sewage and saw their light moving around the walls.

Mike stood up. "How'd you make out, Taylor?"

"All right," he said. "I managed to get a whiff."

"Right then," said Mike. "We better start getting organized."

Stephen held the lamp. The black leather bag was on the floor of the mud chamber. Mike gently plugged the center, eight-inch hole in the base with the gelignite.

He fed the detonator in and then finished off with the putty. "That's it," he said.

They had cleared the tunnel of the lance and the spare rods.

"Go first, one-nine, and back out. I want that light on the wire."

Mike crawled on his side, letting the wire out, careful to see that it didn't drag. He took the wire all the way back to the pontoon and placed the bag next to the detonator box. "Got that sledge, Fagan?" The little man nodded and lifted the short-handled, heavy hammer.

"Bags?" Stephen held them forward.

"I'll bring the phone," Mike said. He turned the mouthpiece. "Cliff? This is it, keep it open. Get Gardner, I'll hold."

The four men stood around the pontoon, eyes alert, muscles tight. Mike was listening. "Good. How's the traffic?" He waited, taking the wires from the bag while he held the telephone receiver under his chin. Taylor stepped forward and took the receiver and held it for him.

"Okay. I want them on the move. Take it from the next red light. Tell me when they change."

The binoculars were an extension of Gardner's eyes, the focus was sharp. They trembled slightly. He held his breath like a marksman before squeezing the trigger. The line of cars and the buses had stopped at the red traffic light at the junction.

Mike wanted to blast as the traffic was revving to pull

away from the lights, so that its noise and vibration would cancel out the explosion.

"Red and amber."

Taylor was on the phone. Mike was at the detonator box. "Let's hope your calculations were right, one-nine," he said.

"Green." Taylor instinctively covered the mouth-piece of the phone with his hand.

Mike counted the sing-song seconds away. "One thousand, two thousand, three thousand."

In the office Gardner mouthed the timing to himself and aimed the binoculars onto the face of the bus driver.

It happened: a muffled roar, then the blast. In the van Cliff thought he heard it as the sound traveled through the sewer and up the shaft. But he couldn't be sure. It might have been his imagination.

The line of traffic kept moving. The bus driver was swearing at the driver of the mini who had cut him off at the lights.

"Move," Mike said.

Fagan went first with the hammer. Then Stephen and finally Mike, clutching the phone and his black leather bag.

The tunnel was thick with dust but the wet from the sewer dampened some of it down. The chamber floor was covered by the rubble of concrete and twisted three-quarter-inch steel. Jagged bars thrust out from the torn edges of the gaping hole in the vault base. Fagan crashed them back with the sledge hammer so that they would not cut themselves going through the hole.

In another part of the City the security company night shift was waiting for their relief to come on duty. They were tired and looking forward to getting home to bed. The day men were never early, unlike the night boys who often turned up an hour before time.

The alarm light on the location board started flashing and buzzing as the first relief man came through the door.

"Christ," said the nightboard operator. "How's that for timing?"

"Hello," said the relief man. "Who's going to take it?"

The night man looked at his watch. "You, mate," he said and stood up, backing away from the insistent light and noise coming from the board.

"Good way to start the day," the relief man said. He checked the code numbers under the light. "Where's the bloody code sheet?" he said.

"In the top righthand drawer, where it always is."

He found the sheet and then the reference. "Bloody hell. It's the City Savings Deposit Bank."

The man at the radio control unit was already calling up the security van.

Stephen stood in the vault. "So this is it," he said.

It was a large rectangular-shaped room and the walls

seemed to be made in a pattern of brushed steel oblongs. At closer range the shapes were lines and lines of deed boxes. Each box had a number plate inset with two neat locks.

The ceiling was also made of steel sheets riveted together at the seams. As he turned to look at the far wall he saw a man standing there staring back at him and he nearly shouted. Then he realized the wall was a mirror of glass and the man was his own image. He had not recognized the dirt-stained, gaunt figure dressed in sewerman's clothes.

In the center concourse of the room were three very large, modern one-ton safes and behind them the high, thick steel bars of the locked, cagelike doors that separated the vault from its massive strong-room door.

"Give us a hand, one-nine."

Mike Daniels' voice startled him, and he turned to help him into the vault. He was still carrying the black bag along with some tools.

"Nice, isn't it?" he said.

"I've never been in one before," said Stephen.

"Well, do the sightseeing tour later. Grab these and start crashing open those boxes. We won't have long to go till old Bill's on the scene."

Mike handed him another chisel and hammer and went over to the wall of deed boxes. "Here goes then. Number seventy, my lucky number."

He put the chisel against the small locks and when he hit it, they snapped away and he pulled the box out of its housing. It was stacked neatly with burgundy-colored velvet bags.

He carried the box to the hole in the vault floor. "You ready, Fagan?" he shouted.

The voice, then Fagan's head, came up to the level of the floor.

"Most of it's cleared away. You know, Taylor even came part way up and gave a hand."

"That's great," said Mike. "Just take this and pass up that phone."

Fagan took the box and disappeared into the chamber.

Stephen had opened his first box. "Looks like a will and the deeds of some house," he said.

"Never mind, just pass it down," Mike told him.

He went to the hole and called out to Fagan. Two hands reached up and took the box from him. As he straightened up, his eyes caught a line of shelves above the flank of boxes along the long wall opposite the entrance.

"Mike," he said. "Look at that."

"What is it?"

"Look. It's cash, shelves of it."

Mike laughed. "I bloody told you they'd have an overspill. The rest of it's in those safes and we're not going to bother with them. Leave it for now and keep going at the boxes, I want to get as many open as we can before the law gets down here."

Stephen picked up his tools and went back to work. "I thought the vault would be soundproof."

"You can't be too sure. With this sort of pressure alarm there's got to be a few air ducts. It's only a chance but they could hear us if we're crashing away."

It took seven minutes for the first security van to arrive.

Four men came out of the back of the van, the senior man from the front passenger seat. The driver stayed at the wheel.

The senior man went to the door of the bank and took a bunch of keys from a chain on his waistband. Gardner watched him unlock the bank but they stood waiting like state troopers in front of a hideout.

Two minutes later the police cars raced up silently. The uniformed men leaped from the cars and the officer with the peaked hat went up to the security man with the keys. They had a quick conference during which another security van turned up. Gardner counted the men—six coppers and eight, nine, ten security men, not counting any of the drivers.

The men got their orders and spread out around the bank building. The officer, a sergeant, two police constables and four of the security boys disappeared into the bank, locking the door behind them.

Gardner turned to the transmitter. "Rover to base."

"Go ahead, Rover."

"Eight passengers just gone to the waiting room."

"Roger, roger Rover, out."

They were working very fast and routinely now. First Mike broke open a box and while he took it to the hole Stephen hammered away, then he took his loot to the hole, by which time Mike was back at the wall, hammering.

The phone on the floor buzzed and they stopped.

"Hello."

Mike listened, his face intent. "Right, Cliff, I got it. What? Yeah, couldn't be better."

"They're in," he said to Stephen. "Eight of 'em."

Stephen put the hammer and chisel gently onto the floor and then moved carefully over to the hole and whispered down to Fagan, "Watch the noise, the police are in the building."

The two of them stood on each side of the hole and stared at each other, ears straining. Mike's face broke into a grin and his voice was low. "We can start packing up them readies now, one-nine."

"Sergeant, you and two men go down and have a look around the vault." The police officer turned to the security official. "Cater, perhaps your men could search the offices, check any windows. You know the form."

The men dispersed and the police officer waited in the hall. The sergeant and two men went down the broad stone steps that led to the basement and the slab of beautiful steel that was the vault door.

The actual door was set into the steel wall, its edges

flush and smooth. A giant hinge in the shape of a waisted letter I ran the whole length of the door. To its left were four small, neat combination locks and a handle like the spokes of a wheel without the rim. To the right of the door in a cavity cut out of the wall was a telephone.

The sergeant went up to the vault door and inspected it. "No sign of any entry here," he said. "Not that anyone'd likely to have got in, but of course you never know, do you?"

"No, sergeant," said one of the police constables.

He went over to the telephone and looked at it. It was an ordinary black telephone.

"Suppose this connects with one inside. Case any fool gets himself locked in," he said by way of explanation to the young constables. "Ah, there's a vault number here." He picked up the receiver and dialed the number.

Inside the vault Mike Daniels' face went white.

Stephen looked as if he were playing statues and the music had stopped.

The ringing went on.

"It's an internal phone, must be for emergencies."

"You're right," Mike said. "Christ, that gave me a turn. Where the hell do they keep it?"

They both concentrated on the ringing.

"It's at the end of that wall," Mike said. "On your side, in the corner."

Stephen went along the wall and saw it resting in an open space at the end of a line of boxes. His reaction to

170

the ringing was so conditioned that he almost lifted his hand to answer it. But then it stopped.

"They must be on the other side of that bleeding door. What about giving 'em a buzz and letting 'em know we're here?"

"Don't joke about it," Stephen said. "I very nearly answered the damn thing."

The sergeant put the receiver back on its cradle. He smiled at the two men. "Didn't actually expect a reply. Still, sometimes what you don't expect turns out to be just what you're looking for. Want to remember that."

The sergeant came back up the stairs and went to report to his superior officer. He told him they had searched the area and inspected the door of the vault and that he had used the emergency telephone. The officer thought it would be advisable if he came down with the sergeant and the security man and had another check, just for the record, in case there were ever any repercussions.

The three men went down to the vault. It didn't look any different to the sergeant. Not a scratch on it.

"Can you open it?" the officer said to the security man.

"Good Lord, no," he said. "Impossible. Unless of course we had authority to burn our way in with a thermic lance. Could be done. But that would ruin a perfectly good vault door."

The officer considered the situation. "Tell me," he said. "Just supposing there was someone in there. Could they get out by opening the door from the inside?"

The security man shook his head. "Not with this model. Some doors maybe, but not this one. No, sir, anyone in there is stuck until Monday morning."

"Make a note of that, sergeant," the officer said. He was obviously thinking ahead to his report. He owed his promotion to his reports.

"I think we had better get the keys to the adjacent buildings," he said. "Resolve the possibility of any digging through. Favorite trick, you know."

"I don't believe there's much chance of that, sir," the security man said. "The walls of that vault are lined with twelve inches of steel."

"Mustn't have it said we didn't cover every avenue of investigation."

"No, sir," the security man said.

The group went back upstairs where the other police and security guards were waiting to report. Negative. No sign of an entry anywhere on the premises.

"Well," the police officer concluded. "We must presume there was a fault in the alarm system. That's for your people to sort out, Cater."

He turned to his sergeant. "Leave two men in the building, sergeant, and arrange a relief rotation. We'll need to be here until the vault is opened on Monday morning."

Gardner counted them as they left the bank. Six,

seven—eight and the officer. The others who had been sniffing around outside were waiting for them. That's it. Sixteen. The lot of them. Another bleedin' conference. Then he saw two of them going back in again.

The policemen got into their cars and pulled away. The security guards were still talking and the man who had the keys was pointing up and down the street to the other buildings.

The sound-powered unit buzzed in the vault and Stephen answered it. "Yes, Cliff. Right, I've got it. Yes, fine. Good-by."

Mike stopped work and waited for Stephen to speak.

"They've gone all right," he said. "But they've left two policemen in the bank."

"Very sensible," Mike said. "Covering themselves. They'll be there till the old jug opens again. Hold this bag. I've nearly finished packing up the readies."

Stephen held the bag for him as he filled it with the bundles of paper money. "Don't take up much room, do they," Mike said. "Not when you consider how much there is. Very convenient bringing out these twenties, fifty sheets of paper to a grand."

Darrin and Kate Daniels stood by the edge of the water throwing pieces of bread at the ducks. "Don't go too near, Kate," Doreen called out. The little girl turned and smiled back at her mother as if to tell her that she knew very well not to fall in and get wet.

Just for an hour, she had thought. She couldn't keep

the kids cooped up in the flat all day while she waited for some word from him. It was hard on them and she wanted to get out, too. The waiting would drive her mad—not knowing what he was doing, how it was going, whether there was trouble. She had finished packing. They were all ready to go. The morning was warm and heavy with thunder clouds. An hour won't hurt, she had thought, before it starts to storm.

Darrin climbed over the low railings that divided the asphalt path from the narrow bank of grass and ran over to the bench seat. He was very sure of himself, like his dad, with fair hair and wide eyes. "All the bread's gone, Mum," he said.

She smiled at him and dug into her carryall for the paper bag. "That's the lot, Darrin," she said. "Give some to Kate. Share it out."

He leaped the railings this time. Mike would have liked seeing that, she thought.

The cry made her look up. "Oh, no," she said. Darrin was holding on to Kate, pulling her out of the water. "I told you not to go too near. What do you think you're doing? Why don't you ever listen?"

Kate was crying and Darrin stood by her with a look of disdain on his face. "I told her, Mum," he said. A feeling of pride came over him. "I got her out, Mum. She would have drowned if I hadn't got her out."

Doreen almost laughed at the drama in his voice, but she let him have his moment of glory. "Come on, we better get back and get you changed."

The little girl looked up at her mother, her tear-filled eyes wide with the innocent guile of her years. "I was feeding them very goodly," she said. "Then I just slipped."

"Come on, let's hurry," Doreen said. "It's starting to rain. There's going to be a storm and we'll all get wet if we're not careful."

Fagan sat in the chamber surrounded by empty deed boxes and assorted plunder. He had sorted out the contents: mounds of jewelry, some loose, some in velvet bags. Then the cash, carefully done up into bundles with elastic or string holding them together: five-pound notes in sealed envelopes. One box had a load of the old white five-pound notes with signatures written on them. So few people passed them in the old days that shopkeepers would insist on the signature.

Then there was a lovely collection of old coins—not to shop with, but nice to keep and maybe one day pop into Sotheby's with.

There were photographs, brown with age, mostly of pretty young women in long summer dresses and big hats. Letters tied together with pictures. Foreign coins, picture postcards, medals, army insignias and all the stuff of memory.

What did they do? he wondered. Come down every once in a while, take them out and dream for a while? Men who had married the other woman and regretted the decision for the rest of their lives, keeping their memories locked up.

The pile of legal documents had overflowed and spilled into the wet mud of the chamber, the red seals stained with the mud of the sewer. Share certificates spoiled, property deeds with their funny squiggle handwriting. Useless to them.

He enjoyed opening the boxes. It was like going to the attic and rummaging through dusty packing cases. Sometimes you would come across a thing of value, something of sentiment. Only for Fagan, there wasn't much sentiment.

Shouldn't be long now, Taylor thought. They've been up there a fair time. Harry was going to be some trouble. He still hadn't moved much and his breathing wasn't very even.

There was nothing he could do until they came down. Then he would help. Mike had pulled it off all right. He was looking forward to sharing it out, seeing how much they'd made.

He sat on the pontoon and opened a bottle of Coke. Only a couple left: just as well they were at the end of it. The water in the sewer was swirling about a bit, he thought.

One of the oxygen bottles that was still leaning against the wall clanged against the pontoon. The sound made Taylor jump. He looked back up the sewer and the water wasn't slow and calm anymore.

He slid off the pontoon into the water. "Christ," he

said. The water was halfway up his thighs and he could feel its pull against his legs. He threw down the Coke bottle and started to wade toward the junction of the other sewer. It wasn't like before, it was bloody hard work.

When he got to the mouth of the tunnel he forgot his fear, but there was a new fear to take its place. The water had risen to the level of the tunnel floor. Pieces of mud fell away and disappeared into the dark thick water. He hesitated for a second, then plunged into the tunnel.

"Mike, Mike." Nobody answered him and he forced himself to crawl farther into the tunnel. "Mike, for Christ's sake, Mike."

"What the fuck's up with you?" Fagan shone the light in Taylor's wild, dirt-streaked face.

"It's the bloody water. It's coming up. The fucking water's coming up the tunnel."

"Jesus." Fagan crawled back into the chamber and scrambled up into the gaping hole of the vault floor.

"Mike," he said. "Taylor says the water's coming up the tunnel."

For the first time Stephen saw fear in Mike's face, white and taut with the knowledge of what was wrong.

He grabbed at the phone and twisted its mouthpiece. "Come on, come on."

"Cliff, get Gardner. Ask him if it's raining."

"What?"

"Get a fucking move on."

They waited, Fagan with his dirt-stained face looking up at them from the hole, Stephen with a half-full bag of money in his hand.

"It's what? Okay."

He slammed the phone back on its cradle. "Everybody out, it's pissing down."

"Do what?"

"I said out. Take what you can, Fagan, and get out, fucking fast."

The little man's head disappeared.

He stuffed his pockets with cash and jewelry, and then looked down the tunnel. "Taylor, you there?"

There was no reply. Fagan started a frantic crawl toward the sewer. Halfway down the tunnel he felt the wet on his hands, seeping through his clothing. He fell out into the sewer and the force of the water knocked him against the wall. He got to his feet and the water buffeted him toward the pontoon.

In the vault Mike worked with calm speed. He had taken a length of rope from around his waist and was tying two of the plastic bags of money together.

"Don't just bloody stand there, one-nine, get a bagful and go. There won't be much fucking time."

He tested the knots, looped the rope over his shoulders and under his arms, then twisted the rope behind so that the two bags rested on his back near the end of his spine.

Stephen did nothing, he just watched.

Mike was ready. "What's the matter with you? Get a

bleeding bag." He said the words deliberately as though he were talking to a child. "There's enough in any one of them to see you right for life."

"I'm not going."

He couldn't believe him. "What do you mean you're not bloody going?"

"What I say. This is the safest place. It won't fill."

"How do you know it won't?"

"I did some research, remember? It won't fill, I'm sure of it."

Mike reached for his black bag. "Maybe you're right. But you don't know it's going to go down either, do you? You might just be sitting here when that door opens on Monday morning."

"You go if you want. I'm staying."

"You're a fool."

"It's better than drowning."

"Yeah?" His hand came out of the black bag clutching a pair of rubber flippers. "Not with these and a mask, mate."

"Good God," said Stephen. "A one-man personal insurance policy. I don't believe it."

The bags of money bounced on his back as he walked to the space in the floor.

"I can't fucking take care of everybody."

"No," Stephen said. "Just you."

He stopped at the hole. "That's right."

Stephen screamed across the vault at him, "What about the others? What about them?"

Mike was standing on the floor of the chamber, his head sticking up into the vault. "There's no fucking time to argue. They knew what they was doing. Are you coming?"

"Fuck off," Stephen said.

Mike smiled at him and tossed the bag through the hole. "In case you change your mind, one-nine, there's another pair in there. Good luck, hope it was worth it."

The bag rolled on its side and Stephen could see the rubber flippers lying in the bottom. He turned back to the hole but Mike was gone.

The water was nearly up to Mike's chest, and it was easier to swim than try to wade and the tide carried him down to the pontoon. The bags of money floated on the water and made their own wave as he dragged them after him.

"Help me, Taylor, for Christ's sake, help me." Fagan had Harry sitting upright on the pontoon but his eyes were glazed and he was not conscious of the panic, the urgency around him.

"Get a mask on," Mike yelled at him. "You got a chance then." He reached the box before Fagan, who now had to grip tight to the pontoon to stop himself from being swept away by the rush of water.

Mike took a set for himself and threw first one then another across the distance between them. The small bottles of air swung wildly and the little man clutched at the mask but the bottles hit him in the chest and he lost one of the units in the water. Mike pulled a third set from the container. "Watch it, Fagan, here it comes." Fagan caught it.

Where the fuck's Taylor? he thought and then he saw him. He couldn't call out because he had the mask firmly in position now. But there was nothing he could have done. Taylor was screaming and clawing at the brick and mud column. His arms thrashed wildly but he could not hold onto the mud or climb on it. He looked like one of those long distance swimmers who covered themselves in grease to keep out the cold sea.

Mike turned back to the junction and submerged under the water. It was pitch black and he was a blind man with only his sense of touch to guide him. He ripped off the protective gloves and fought against the pull of the water, his hands searching, feeling. Then he found it, a thin, strong line gently swaying in the water like the tail of a fish.

He came up and as his head broke the surface he saw it coming. It was like a slow gentle wave that was breaking onto a beach. It glided over the water pushing ahead of it bouncing Spiralarm lamps that it had ripped from the hooks in the wall of the sewer.

Fagan was trying to get the mask over Harry's face when the curve of the wave hit the pontoon. For an instant it seemed to hold. Then it was ripped from its supports. Harry tumbled into the water, his face pitiful and devoid of understanding. His limp body crashed and bumped against oxygen cylinders and floating plastic crates. He took the little man who had stayed to help under the water with him and then the pontoon crushed down on them. It turned over and their bodies were lifted up to the ceiling of the sewer.

The water hit Taylor and pressed him into the mud column, cutting off his screams, enveloping him. The pressure of the water shot him up the shaft he had been trying to climb. By then he was finished, his lungs full of the stinking rain water and foul matter of the sewage.

Mike Daniels clutched at the phone line and let the force of the water take him. He felt his body being battered by the debris of their equipment but he held fast to the line. It was a chance, the only one in that swirling black tube twenty feet under the City of London. It was a life line that could lead him to safety. He hoped the kid was still there.

In the vault Stephen waited. He could hear the rush of water and smell the stench of the sewage it was stirring up. He wished he hadn't been short with Mike but it was too late now: the flood would have taken them all. He should have known Mike wouldn't give, not him. This was his job, his brain child. Nobody else could tell him what to do. They don't have a chance, Stephen thought.

Now there was just him and the two above ground. They'd wait, he supposed, and then they would have to leave since there would be nothing else they could do.

Gardner in the office watching the rain and Cliff in the van, sitting at the table looking at the phone, waiting for it to ring.

Well, he'd better think about himself. He wasn't out of it by a long way. He searched his pockets and found a pencil, but nothing to write on. Everything was wet, except the money. He laughed. There was more of that than anything else.

He paced out the length and breadth of the vault, guessing the height, and then he sat down on one of the empty deed boxes and started to do his calculations. The problem was that there were too many imponderables: how much water, its velocity? The air content of the vault—that he could work out—should be enough to last, to Monday morning if needs be.

The cubic capacity of the tunnel he knew, but how would the water behave? He got his answer. There was a gurgling at the hole and then the water seeped over the edge and into the vault. It did not come in a rush, but more like the water that appears under the door of a bathroom when someone has left the plug in and the taps running.

It spread slowly over the floor and through the bars of the cage doors and up to the thick, watertight vault door, washing up the scattered money they had dropped. It took time but it kept rising.

His stomach was empty and he remembered he hadn't eaten since the last sandwich early that morning. It really is too much, he thought. Sitting here with all that damn money, nowhere to go, nothing he could spend it on.

It would be a funny sight when they opened the doors. They'd get wet—that was one thing. If the water kept rising he could always lie on the shelves, they went nearly to the ceiling.

All that planning and trouble and work. God, it had been hard going. At least he'd be famous. That was some consolation. Perhaps if the rain stopped he'd have a chance. But he didn't know how long it would take for the water to go down. There was a hell of a lot of it.

He felt sorry for Mike and Harry. The others didn't matter too much. He hadn't got close to them. Harry was a funny man, and you always liked a man who could make you laugh.

The plastic bags of money started to float on the water. Wonder how much there's in them? he thought. If one small packet was a thousand, it was a fortune all right. How many packets to a bag? Fifty, a hundred? Maybe more. Two bags wouldn't be heavy to carry and they would take care of him for life, only there was nowhere to carry them.

The sewers from the City wind their way underground for about four miles to a pumping station called Abbey Mills whose screen rises from the sewer like the steel bars of a cage. Its purpose is to stop large pieces of debris from filtering into the station and gumming up the works.

The system is automatic and very modern. A machine that looks like a giant garden rake sweeps down over the screen and into the sewage. The teeth go between the bars of the screen and then lift, bringing with them anything stuck there, and deposit it into a hopper.

Sometimes if a piece of wood or metal is too large the screen will freeze and a man is sent into the sewer with a lamp to find out what it is that has stopped the screen from operating.

The screen stopped suddenly at lunchtime on Saturday. The man in charge took his lamp and went down into the sewer. What the bloody hell, he said to himself. There were crates and crushed sections of thick sheeting that were like a raft. He waded into the sewage and put his hands into the liquid. He felt something soft. The matted head of a man gently floated to the top of the water.

The man clutched at the bars of the screen and vomited in the sewage.

Two other bodies were found later in the day.

EPILOGUE

If you live in Wimbledon you have a chance to see the seasons changing. Jennifer Booker was going to miss it. The furniture van came on the dot at eight that morning. It was cold without the heating and she wore her sheepskin coat as she helped the men. She didn't want them breaking the glass-framed pictures.

"Good morning, madam." It was the postman. "Off today then?"

"Yes," she said. "I've sent the form in so that the mail gets forwarded," she told him.

"Well, good luck," he said. "Where you going to?"

"Oh, out of London," she said.

He handed her the post and then walked on up the street.

She went slowly back into the house that, now emptied, took on a hollow sound and opened the mail. Christmas catalogues already.

There was a picture postcard. Funny time to get a postcard of a beach, she thought.

She called up the stairs. "Darling, who do we know in Australia?"

AFTERWORD

I never intended writing this book.

I don't need the money—anymore. I certainly don't want the publicity and I'm not worried about my family. The girls are grown up now anyway. I suppose I didn't want to tempt fate. But then one evening I met this man.

We were in a bar and since it was obvious we were both English we got talking and drinking and eventually as the evening and the liquor wore on, the story came out. When you've been through something like I have, it is very difficult not to talk about it when you feel you have the companionship of someone you trust.

He thought the story was fantastic and he remembered reading about it in the newspapers. They got it wrong, of course, but then they didn't have all the facts. I did. That was what made the whole thing so compelling to him.

It was then he told me he was a book publisher. He became very persuasive and he knew how to appeal to my ego. He guaranteed complete protection as well as a very interesting deal and I thought, well, maybe if I used a pseudonym and changed the other names around it would be rather a kick seeing the books in the libraries and in the shops and at airports. (We do quite a bit of traveling now.) And it did seem too good a story to keep hidden away forever, particularly as it was a true one.

So that was it, really.

I had to tell Jennifer about it after a while, and surprisingly, she not only understood but was rather excited. She even became involved in reading and correcting the book proofs. Her only disappointment was that she never had met Mike Daniels.

The amazing thing was that she didn't think what I had done was immoral. "It wasn't like breaking into somebody's house," she had said. I suppose that is a very feminine way of looking at it, rather than male logic which would conclude that stealing is stealing, whatever it might be.

Maybe it is because robbing an institution like a bank is so impersonal. She said it was because it was so clever and daring.

The only awful thing was what happened to Taylor, Fagan and Harry. The other two, Cliff and Gardner, were given their share and I believe they set up a boutique together in the south of France. I bet they're having a fine old time down there in the tourist season.

As you will have guessed the water level in the vault that day did go down—quite quickly, actually—and all I had to do was pick up the two full bags of twenties and the best of the jewelry and walk out along the sewer to the shaft where the van was. They were still waiting because the rain had stopped and Mike saw that I would probably have a good chance.

One final note of caution. If any of you has thoughts about doing your own bank vault I should warn you that the police, the security firms and the banks will have read this book too. From what I hear, the appropriate security arrangements have now been made so it would be rather risky to duplicate our little caper.

We still look forward to getting our annual card from Australia. Mike sends it on our anniversary—of the job, that is.

Stephen Booker
Acapulco, 1972.